Lady A

Cassie M. Shiels

DEDICATION

To my handsome Prince! I love you John!

Other novels by Cassie M. Shiels

The Royal Spy (A Princess tale 1)

Lady A (A Princess Tale 2)

The Prince's Decoy (A Princess Tale 3)

Coming soon! The Queens of Adelfa series.

Chapter 1

~Lady A~

I knew I looked like a fool—wringing my hands and walking in circles as my long skirts gathered small clumps of dirt. I stopped my hasty steps long enough to stare down the road but it was empty. I knew it was dangerous to be out on the road all alone, but I could no longer stand sitting inside listening to my own heartbeat in my ears. That was torture.

At every crunch of a carriage wheel on the gravel, or laugh of the children playing in the village, my stomach tightened. I doubted the mad man Manic and his brutal, black-cloaked riders would swoop down and end my life at this moment. Apparently, no one else in Veyon thought so either, but that fate was a real possibility. I knew that more than most.

I looked down both sides of the tree-lined road. I frowned. There was no sign of my brother, Dan. Two boys with wooden swords and rough leather armor raced past, both declaring they'd be knighted before the other. Their game made the corners of my mouth twitch into a slight smile, but the tightness in my stomach grew. I watched them disappear into their thatched roof cottage under the stern motherly gaze of the woman at the door. Manic wasn't one to spare children if they got in his way. It was better for them to be home.

The wind picked up its speed, and I rubbed my arms in an attempt to ward off the chill. I looked down the road again, but all I could see were trees, rocks, and sagging black clouds.

Thunder rumbled overhead. With a flash of lightning, my hands started shaking on their own. I clasped them together to stop the trembling.

"Come on, Dan," I mumbled into the wind. I tried to convince myself that he had said late afternoon in his letter instead of early afternoon, but I was unsuccessful. He had been clear.

I pulled my long, brown hair around my shoulder and started braiding, keeping my eyes on the road. Nothing. I let go of my braid and threw it over my shoulder. This was no time to worry in earnest. Dan had been acting as a spy for three weeks and had not been caught. I could not start losing faith in him. My brother would be fine. He was a knight, trained to handle difficult situations. Something had simply held him up. Not Manic-related. I hoped.

I gulped and tried not to imagine him fighting a circle of black-cloaked thugs; who thought they deserved to rule the country with Manic as their rightful king. They showed no mercy to anyone who said otherwise. Dan said otherwise. If Dan were discovered, they would kill him without a second thought.

"My Lady," our steward, Hewitt, called from behind me as the first drops of rain began to fall. "I think it might be best if you came in."

"Just a few moments more, Hewitt. Dan is bound to be here any second."

"Your brother wouldn't want you out here shivering like a wet kitten, My Lady."

I thought about pointing out to him that it had been *Dan* who had often dragged me, kicking and screaming, out of our manor into the rain when we were young. But he knew that as well as I. Hewitt offered me his arm as the wind picked up speed, making my long sleeves fly about as if they wanted to rip free of my dress and fly away to a safer kingdom. With one last look down the empty road, I nodded and allowed him to escort me back to the old, stone manor.

Thunder boomed like cannon fire, even louder than a few minutes before. The wind increased, making the willow trees lining our rocky lane shake in an angry dance. Hewitt picked up his speed and I matched his pace; racing through the front door just in time to beat the deluge. I looked back and squinted through the curtain of rain wishing Dan was somehow behind us, but all I could see was rain and wet leaves. Hewitt closed the door with a knowing look.

"I am positive something held him up, My Lady. Perhaps he's been forced to take shelter somewhere because of this storm." I nodded and let out the breath that must have been stuck in my lungs. I trudged up the main stairs to my sitting room. I didn't know if I should be angry with Dan or scared. Both emotions battled equally strong.

If only Prince James, my brother's best friend, could have convinced Dan out of this ridiculous idea. But James had been part of this latest idiotic plan—the worst one of all of Dan's crazy schemes. No matter what I said to Dan, or wrote in my letters to James, I couldn't convince either of them to see reason.

Even though we had never met face-to-face, Prince James and I had made a great team, for the last two years, keeping Dan out of trouble. We had always been on the same side, why not this time?

How they had convinced me to take a part in their plan, I still don't know. Maybe I agreed so I could attempt to control the uncontrollable. Maybe I too wanted to end the fear Manic had spread throughout the land with his claims to our kingdom. Regardless, I could not wait until this was all over and I was no longer required to keep Manic's secrets Dan kept collecting.

I took to pacing my upstairs sitting room and wishing my parents were here. But as ambassadors to the crown, they were away more often than not. They would be gone to Uree, the country across the sea, for about three months more, and I knew that even if I wrote to them this very second, I would not hear back for at least a month. Dan was hoping they would never find out what sort of danger he had placed himself in. At least, not until it was over.

I took turns looking out the window and pacing the floor. When I realized I was driving myself mad, I pulled a book off of the shelf. Not even glancing at the cover, I flipped through it. But, I found I couldn't focus on any of the words. I finally tossed it aside and pulled out my embroidery, mumbling as I stabbed the muslin much harder than usual.

I nearly stabbed my finger when a knock sounded on the door.

"Come in," I said tossing the shambolic embroidery aside.

Mrs. Carlton, our housekeeper, came in holding a small white letter. "The poor boy that delivered this is soaked through. He said he would wait by the fire for your reply. Perhaps you could give him enough time to eat some hot soup?"

I recognized the Prince's handwriting right away and felt my heart leap in my chest. I accepted the slightly damp letter with a smile. "Give him a nice big bowl," I said.

She nodded and walked to the door, but paused with her hand on the doorknob. "Are you all right, My Lady?"

"Yes, why?"

"Well, it looks like you have hastily braided your hair at least half a dozen times."

I laughed, glancing at my tangled hair, "You know me far too well."

She smiled, "That I do, My Lady. Now stop your fretting. Your brother will be here soon. It will take more then a little rain to stop a stalwart knight like him."

That's what I am afraid of, I thought as she left. I sat down at my writing desk and slit open the Prince's letter.

"My Dear Lady A," it started.

I smiled as I always did at that salutation. I had never told him my first name and I loved it when he guessed it wrong—which he did in every letter. His family, and mine, adored this game we had accidentally created, and everyone who knew my name refused to tell him. I knew Dan was very convincing on the subject. James pretended to be distraught and anxious, but I knew he enjoyed it too. Having never met, only corresponding through letters, our game had lasted these last two years. It did help that for a year of that time I was far away in the country of Thion with my parents.

> My Dear Lady A,
> I know Dan is going to return to report again today. I cannot take the mystery anymore. You said what Dan has discovered is unsafe to put in a letter, so I am coming to hear about it myself. Yes, in person. I should arrive this evening. I hope you will be there so we can finally meet face to face. I will admit to an ulterior motive—I plan to finally learn your name. It isn't Angelique is it?
> Truly yours,
> James

I reread his letter two more times to make sure I had not imagined his words. Prince James was coming to meet me? I sat back in my chair and breathed out slowly, not sure how I felt about that. I did want to meet him. I always had. But I couldn't bring myself to actually allow it to happen.

Our letters were safe. Through our letters I was brave, beautiful, and his ideal girl. I could safely romanticize that we were courting. But if we actually met—what if that dream was destroyed? What if he took one look at me and decided that I was not worthy? I knew I feared the court more than anything else, and that would be unacceptable for him. He was the Prince; his life was at the castle.

I had imagined him riding up to my house and pulling me into my arms a million times. But it had only been a dream, a fantasy of something that would never happen, because I would not let it. I was too afraid he would reject me like the other courtiers had. I was too afraid that I would disappoint him somehow, and I would be left alone with only my shattered heart and enough tears to fill a soup pot.

I couldn't risk it. I ran to my desk, pulled out a new piece of parchment and a quill. I scrawled what I knew was a thin excuse. I knew he would see right through it. I froze, rereading my words, the quill suspended in the air watching the ink dry.

I shook my head. *No.* It had been two years of letters. If I was honest with myself, I wanted to actually hear his voice, see his face, and give us a chance. A different kind of nervousness ran up my arms and settled into my chest, competing with my worry for Dan. I crumpled my letter as I decided I would do it. I would meet James. I had to.

I threw my hair around, quickly braided it properly, took a deep breath, and pulled out a fresh sheet of parchment. If I was more afraid of meeting the Prince than I was of Manic, his men, and the possible horrendous fate of my brother, then I was a fool. I pushed my anxious thoughts to the back of my mind and wrote my reply before I lost my nerve:

Dear Prince James,

I guess a meeting between us all would be best. I will try to make sure that I am available. I know you are smiling at that last statement and if not you are smiling now. There is so much to tell you— the biggest thing is that we are fairly sure we know how to stop him. I might have been wroth with this foolish plan at first, but it seems you and Dan were right, this once. That is if Dan makes it home soon. If not, I will be more than wroth with you. Something I assure you; you do not want. No, Angelique is wrong too, guess again!

Your friend,

Lady A

I stared at the words "Your friend" as the ink dried. I thought about signing it differently, but if he was coming here, I didn't want either of us to jump to conclusions. I sealed the letter and put it in my apron pocket. I knew Mrs. Carlton would come for it after she was satisfied with the messenger boy's well-being. At this point, it would probably be delivered as the Prince rode up our drive.

I half-heartedly looked out the window, not wanting to feel disappointed again. There was still no sign of Dan. I moaned, sat back down, and started pulling the messy stitches out of my embroidery.

The crash of the front door a few moments later made me stab my finger with the needle. "Ouch!" I said shaking it to stop the stinging, but the pounding of footsteps on the stairs made me pause. I didn't like how they sounded—rushed, urgent even.

Dan threw the door open and stood there with his arms on the frame breathing heavily. He was dripping wet and covered in mud.

I jumped up. "Dan! Are you all right?"

He slowly raised his eyes to mine; the look I saw there caused a shiver to run down my arms and prickle my skin. I pulled my arms tight to my chest, attempting to stop the cold feeling from spreading.

"You have to get out of here, now!" he gasped.

"Dan, what happened?"

He shook his head and looked at the floor.

"Tell me!"

"There is no time, they are coming for you." His eyes left the floor and rose to the curtains. "The window…" he said as he rushed forward and looked outside.

"Why me?"

He turned his eyes back on the floor. "I made a mistake. I should have listened to you. James and I thought this was the only way to bring Manic down. But it's not worth your life."

"Dan?"

"No, don't try to tell me it's not my fault. I didn't mean to mention you; it was an accident, it slipped out. And now Manic has it in his crazy, bloodthirsty head, that to prove my ultimate loyalty to his traitorous group…I have to allow them to kill you."

My heart stopped. "Why?!"

He ran his hands through his hair and leaned against the wall, letting the water and mud drip onto the rug. "He wants solid proof that I am one of them, now that I know his identity."

"You've met him, for sure? Not a decoy?"

"Yes, and it was not a privilege, but it was who I told you I suspected. We will need to describe him to James right away so the patrols know who they are looking for specifically."

He looked over at me and jumped as if he had been pricked and looked back out the window, only to clench his jaw. "Quick! They are coming, and I can't fight them all!" he said as he raced to the sitting room door and closed it. "I will hold them off while you run," he said returning to the window.

"Dan, you can't. You'll be killed!"

"They don't know I am a spy. If you are simply not here when they arrive maybe they won't..." He huffed. "Come on," he said as he pushed open the window, and waved me over. I numbly stumbled over to him.

"Dan, James is coming here." Dan froze, his hand on the windowsill. "He said he would be here by nightfall."

Dan looked out at the dark skies. "Then we have no more time." He took his dark blue cloak off and tied it around me. Dan's face grew tight, and he turned me to face him directly.

"I told you everything I have learned these past few weeks so you must head directly to Saris and tell James and the King everything. I am trusting you to do this." I opened my mouth, but he didn't let me speak. "Only you can deliver this message. Only you can stop this."

"Dan I can't. I can't go there, not after what happened at court. I can't go back! I vowed never to go back to the castle."

He glanced out the window one more time, "You have to. You cannot let silly things from your childhood get in the way anymore. I'm sorry, but if you don't, Manic will win. You have to put your fears aside. Tell James everything about the specifics of Manic's plans. Make sure he knows that in sixteen days Manic means to attack the castle in Saris."

"Sixteen days? Are you sure?"

"Yes, it's important to him that he takes over the Kingdom on that day. I don't know why for sure, but I could guess."

A loud knock on the door downstairs made my throat go dry.

"If James is on his way here, meet him on the road. I know we have enough information to stop Manic, but only if you get out of here now. Let nothing stop you." He unfastened the curtains and pushed the window all the way open. "Come on."

I numbly nodded, hoping that I would meet James on the road and wouldn't have to go to Saris at all. Dan extended his hand, and helped me onto the windowsill. I eyed the wet ledge below me, and looked back at my brother.

"You can do it. You only have to be brave for a moment, one moment," he said, nodding to the ledge. "It's this or let Manic kill you."

I took a deep breath and followed the ledge with my eyes to where the Beech tree's branches brushed it. I gulped, silently counted to three, then eased out of the window carefully setting my feet down on the wet ledge. The water instantly soaked through my shoes.

Loud voices filled the hall outside my sitting room and Dan yanked the curtains closed as the door burst open. I carefully moved along the damp ledge toward the tree, trying not to cry.

"Sir Daniel, what a nice manor you have," laughed a voice in my sitting room. "The pleasures of being a Noble and a Knight I wager."

"I'm glad you approve Manic," my brother stammered. "It has been in our family for six generations."

"And you want to give up all of this?" said the voice. "For me?"

"I told you none of this matters to me, and besides I know you reward your followers. I don't doubt I'll get it back."

"Ah... so you think this house will be your reward. Perhaps you are right, we shall see."

"Can I get you anything to eat?" my brother asked, his voice remarkably steady.

I knew he was trying to give me enough time to get away. I reached out and touched the slippery tree. I wished at that moment that James was here to help, but even if he left the castle when he sent the letter, he'd still be a fair distance away. Taking a deep breath, I put my foot on the tree.

"You know what I want, Dan."

"I'm afraid I don't know your preference, though I do have an excellent cook."

A harsh laugh rent the air, nearly making me slide as I placed my other slipper on the wet tree branch.

"Always playing the Court Jester, Dan, but that's why I like you. We are here to celebrate you. You're officially joining the group."

I heard loud cheers as I slipped down the tree.

"That is, after we take care of one little thing. Where is she, Dan?"

My foot slipped and I fell the last few feet landing in a pile of leaves that the storm had swept under the tree. My heart pounding in my ears and a crack of thunder made me miss my brother's reply.

I knew I couldn't wait around and listen to more, so I rolled out of the leaves and raced to the stables. My brother's horse, Narcissus, stood munching hay, still saddled. *Where were the stable hands? Hopefully still at dinner,* I thought. The alternative was that Manic's men had already taken care of them. You were a follower or you were dead. I looked from Narcissus to my own horse, Mabel, and sighed. Narcissus was far too strong of a horse for me, but he was all ready to go. The first angry shouts from the house reached my ears, and made my decision.

Please be okay, Dan, I thought as I pulled Narcissus around. If I was quick enough maybe James and I could come back to help him.

I climbed up on the stall to help me mount, and guided him out of the stables into the rainy yard. Quietly, I rode Narcissus around the house toward our rocky drive. A scream of pain that cut through the howl of the wind made me pull back on the reins. I looked up at the upstairs window and felt as if I had been hit in the chest.

An unsightly looking, black, hairy face was there laughing. "There she is, Master Manic."

"Let's go Narcissus!" I yelled. We took off down our drive, making the willows sway as we passed. I tried not to think about Dan, or what might have happened to him. But I couldn't stop a tear or two from slipping down my cheek. *Get to James*, I told myself. *He will know what to do.*

The sound of horses somewhere behind me made me wrap the reins tighter around my wrists and urge Narcissus to run faster. A moment later, though, they were not far behind me. I knew I couldn't outrun them on the road, so I steered Narcissus into the trees to try and lose them in the foliage. I let him lead us through while I clenched my thighs to try and stay on. I looked for the river that I knew would eventually lead me to the road toward Saris, but I couldn't focus on much at the speed we were going.

Trembling I reined Narcissus in to slow him at the same moment an arrow whizzed through the air and embedded itself in a tree a few feet to my right. I screamed, and I clamped my own hand over my mouth. No other arrows followed. Shouts of triumph echoed behind me. They had used arrows to find me. I urged Narcissus to take flight again as fast as we could go while dodging trees.

I had to hold on tight so as not to be thrown off, but even as fast as we were going, I could still hear them gaining. *Maybe the road would have been better*, I thought. Narcissus was the best horse in the land, but perhaps the trees were getting in the way.

My thighs where throbbing by the time the trees began to thin and I caught sight of the river. The men's hoots and ugly laughter sounded only a few yards behind me. "Come on!" I yelled to my horse.

We found a trail and began to gallop along the edge of the rapid rain-clogged river that was starting to sink deeper into the earth. I knew it fell into a ravine not far ahead; I hoped I could find a good place to cross it before it did. I caught sight of a green hill devoid of trees. The road to Saris was up on top. I knew there was no way I would beat them up that hill. Nor did I have time to find a way to safely cross the river. Suddenly I felt trapped, and the icy hand of fear wrapped around my heart and squeezed.

The twang of an arrow made me forget about the pain in my thighs for a moment as it whizzed by nearly nicking my shoulder.

"I've got her if you want her, Master Manic!" one of his men shouted.

"Not yet," he laughed. "I am enjoying this." The whole group whooped. "Spread out men. Let's see if she will be a good little sheep."

I felt tears streaming down my cheeks, mixing with the rain, as the icy hand of fear returned to its squeezing. I looked around for any kind of escape—there had to be a bridge or something—but there wasn't. I had no choice; the river churned five feet down from the ledge.

I yanked Narcissus' head around so he would head straight for the river, but he turned his head back. The reins burned my hands, but I forced his head around again. He obeyed for a moment, but right at the river's edge he suddenly squealed and reared up.

I couldn't hold on and fell to the damp ground. Pain exploded in my wrist and my backside. I found for a moment that I could hardly breathe. Narcissus took off, an arrow in his hindquarters. I looked around for an escape; across the river there was a light. It was the only hope I had. The man who I now knew was Manic started laughing, his wild orange hair poofed out like a lion's mane. He got off his horse and drew his sword.

"It will be my pleasure to kill you, My Lady. I always prefer to do the important ones myself instead of one of my men. Though, in this particular case, I would have preferred your own brother to do the job. However, a good leader must set the example for his men."

Seeing no other option, to save my own life, I pushed hard against the wet ground and threw myself into the river. The frigid water enveloped me and I gasped for breath as my head surfaced for a moment only to be drug back down under the churning water. I tumbled through the river a few times before I felt my head bang against something hard, and then I knew no more.

Only darkness.

Chapter 2

~James~

My horse, Dante, seemed to sense my unease as we fought our way through the wind. We kept a close eye out for Manic and his men as we traveled to Veyon, but I knew his men would stay away from us. Manic kept saying he was going to take over the Kingdom, but in his own time. Patrols were continually being sent out. Unfortunately, so far, none had yet to apprehend him.

Manic's men always dropped whatever terror they were inflicting and ran like the cowards they were when we were with in eyesight. None of his followers seemed willing to give up any information on Manic when we did catch them. That's why Dan's plan had to be successful.

With all of us wearing the dark blue cloaks and silver chainmail that marked us as knights of Salvina, they were bound to stay hidden.

Not many people knew Dan was spying on Manic. We didn't want Manic to suspect Dan was not true to his betrayal of the country and me. Not even our friends, my most trusted of knights, knew until this afternoon—even then I was loathed to have chosen them for this venture. The greater number of people involved, the greater the danger for Dan.

On the other hand, I didn't need to be teased by any of my other men. As much as I said this trip was all about Manic, I honestly wanted to meet Lady A more. My friends knew of our letters of course, and their teasing was guaranteed even if I had left them behind.

A part of me wished Manic and his black-cloaked men would attack us so I could work out some of my tenseness. It was deranged how much more concerned I was to meet Lady A than I was about meeting up with Manic's men.

I nudged my horse forward so I was riding even with Richard, my faithful bodyguard. I kept my focus only on the muddy road and the shadows in the thick trees all around us.

"We should be seeing Veyon soon," I said knowing full well I sounded like I was trying to make small talk.

Richard thankfully didn't laugh, but kept his reaction to a simple smile.

"Yes, James, we should."

"You're not nervous, are you?" asked Roland bringing his horse even with mine and rolling his hazel eyes as dramatically as possible.

"Why would I be?" I asked, as Edgar, Frederick, and Darwin pulled their horses as close to us as they could.

"Come on James," laughed Edgar pushing his dark brown hair out of his eyes. "You can't hide it from us. We know you too well."

"You have been dying to meet her for months," added Darwin clasping his brown hands together and fluttering his eyelashes.

"Its true, you can't trick us into thinking this is some secret mission," said Roland.

"We all know this is about her," added Frederick, as he attempted to curl his blond beard with his fingers.

"All right, men, leave him alone," cut in Richard. They all laughed and resumed their quiet watchfulness. With Manic's men on the loose, even if we didn't think they would attack us, we couldn't afford to be distracted, that was the surest way to get an arrow in our skulls. After a few moments of silence, I was able to push off thoughts of Lady A for the time being.

We rode down Veyon's deserted wet streets well after dark. We had set out later than I had intended, but I was sure my letter would have arrived earlier that afternoon. I could imagine Dan, with his usual, crazy energy, pacing with the excitement of his scheme actually working. But I hoped his sister would be awake when we arrived. This was my best chance to see her.

We turned down the Albon's long drive, and my heartbeat increased with every step. The wet willows sprinkled us with water as we rode past. But when I saw the house, I felt my muscles tense. I reined in Dante, and my knights put their hands on their matching silver swords.

Dan wasn't bounding down the steps with a triumphant smile on his face, waving a victory torch, ready to tell of his adventures; in fact, there were no lights in the house at all. A small tremor ran through me. *Why were there no lights?*

"Men, be on guard," I said drawing my sword and leaping off my black warhorse. I swallowed a few times to try and get rid of the dry feeling in my throat, but it did nothing. When we reached the house and saw that the door was ajar, I clenched my teeth and waved my men forward.

"Edgar, Darwin, and Richard, on my right," I breathed as I slowly approached the door. "Frederick, Roland, my left." Holding my sword aloft, I kicked the door open. No sounds or movement of any kind followed.

"I don't like it," I muttered as I shot a glance at my men. Their faces reflected my own. I waved them forward, and we crept inside.

We were only a few feet inside when Richard nudged my arm. "James."

I looked at him but he pointed to the floor. In the torchlight streaming in from the door was Hewitt, the Albon's steward, lying in his own blood. My blood began racing through my veins as it only did during a fight.

"Frederick, Roland, take the right hall. Edgar, Darwin, the left," I said as I darted to the main staircase, knowing Richard would follow me, as any good bodyguard would.

We searched the upper rooms, but found nothing and no one—not even a servant. The house felt haunted. I hoped no one else had been made a ghost. But no other bodies suggested that.

"This doesn't feel right, Richard."

"I know."

"Dan! Lady A?" I finally called. No voice answered but my own echoing in the cold, empty halls. I leaned against the wall and tried to think clearly through the extra blood rushing to my heart. I took a few deep breaths to regain my calm demeanor. I looked up to give Richard a confident nod, but I caught sight of a painting lit by Richard's torchlight and my breath froze. I was starring right at a pair of blue-gray eyes.

"James?" asked Richard, but I had no response. I took a step closer to the portrait. Dan was standing next to Lord and Lady Albon, but it was the girl (who looked like a younger version of Lady Albon) that kept me staring. Her hair was dark like Dan's, but her blue-gray eyes were all her own.

"James," said Richard again, and I pulled my eyes away.

"We have to find them," I said as I turned away from the portrait and marched down the hall. We met my other knights back downstairs. But I knew their disappointing news before they spoke it.

"Nothing," said Edgar.

"Same," said Frederick.

"Let's try the stables," I said as I sprinted out the door, but I had little hope that anyone was there.

We rushed out into the night, but the stables were empty of human life as well. I looked at the horses closely, but I didn't see Narcissus, Dan's horse. As far as I could tell he could have never arrived home.

"What do you think happened, here?" Edgar asked.

"James do you think…" started Darwin.

"No, I can't think it was him."

"What else could have happened?" asked Frederick.

"I am not sure," I said. "But we will find out. Search the woods and the town. I want to know the moment any of you find so much as a hint of a clue." I paused not wanting to voice it, but I had to. "And if Manic did this so help me, he will pay... let's go!" I yelled racing to my own horse.

I didn't dare let my mind dwell on what could have happened, but forced my thoughts to what had to be done.

Richard followed me as I steered Dante into the woods. I was glad to see my other knights heading toward town. We would find them. We had to find them.

* * * *

A few hours later, nearly frozen from the cold wind, Richard and I returned to the house. "We had better get some rest, James," he said. I sighed knowing he was right. The others had returned and had nothing to report. We all agreed that in the light of the morning things would be easier.

We slept in the stable; I couldn't bring myself to invite ourselves into the house. My knights slept soundly, but I could not. Thoughts of Manic torturing Dan and Lady A made it impossible. No, I wouldn't let myself imagine them dead. I focused on the face I saw in the painting—her eyes smiling at me—and squeezed my eyes tight.

Once the inky, black sky began to turn slightly blue, I arose and went back into the house. I hesitated in the entrance hall and looked at Hewitt. He was stabbed only once right through his heart. I could imagine Manic barging in and stabbing the poor man without a second thought before casually walking further into the house. I stopped myself before I thought of what could have happened next and focused only on fact.

I pulled a curtain down to cover Hewitt; we would take care of him later. I searched every room again myself. Richard found me in the upstairs sitting room after the sun had risen. I was crouched down staring at the wet rug by the window where there was a small circle of blood. I didn't look up at Richard as he knelt down beside me.

"Embroidery on the couch," I said. "And on the desk is my letter."

"Don't go there, James. She will be all right. That blood is little more than what a broken nose could produce."

"Is it?"

I wanted to believe him but didn't think I could. I had promised Lady A nothing would happen and that this crazy plan of her brother's was a good one. She had tried to convince us to think of something else, anything else, but we had not listened. Now she was missing, possibly dead.

"We will find her, James. And Dan."

I sighed and stood, "Then let's go find them. There is nothing else for us here."

We went outside where I accepted some bread and cheese from Frederick and climbed back onto Dante. "Let's move."

We searched the village and much of the surrounding woods, but found nothing significant. By noon we started heading north, back toward Saris. I wasn't about to give up. But we needed more men if we were to comb the entire wood, or better yet, find a way to chase Manic down and force him tell us where they were, by what ever means I deemed necessary.

We were almost to Avern, a small town between Veyon and Saris, when we intercepted a messenger.

"Noble Knights, I am looking for the Prince. Is he with you?" a young man called from his horse waving a letter like a white flag. "I have a message for him."

"Yes, I am here," I said nudging Dante forward.

The messenger boy did the same and bowed his head when we were side by side.

"Your Highness, this was sent for you."

I snatched the letter as Richard tossed the young man a coin. I was fully expecting it to be from Lady A explaining that she and Dan were safe at the castle, but it wasn't her handwriting on the front. I let out the breath I had been holding and opened the letter.

> Your Royal Highness, Prince James,
>
> We do not wish to trouble you, but we believe we have a friend of yours here at our Inn in Avern—The Old Wheel Inn. She is badly hurt and in need of more assistance then we think we can give. We don't know any of the magic of healing that we have heard the Royal healers possess, but we do believe she is in need of it.

We assume you know her because of a letter
we found on her person. We are unsure of her name
but her letter was signed Lady A.

Forgive us for reading it, but it was the only
clue we had. If you could send the appropriate person
for her, we would appreciate it. We will care for her
until we hear from you.
Your humble servants,
Charles and Wendy

I shoved the letter into Richard's hands and kicked
Dante into a gallop.

She was alive.

Chapter 3

~Lady A~

The first thing I registered was pain coursing through every inch of me. My head felt like there was a small, pounding hammer inside my skull and my eyes felt like they had been filled with sand and sewn shut with a rusty needle. For a moment all I could focus on was the pain. But as I lay there, I was able to come to terms with it enough to attempt opening my eyes.

It took a few tries before they creaked open; I was met with a blinding light and quickly shut them. I took a steadying breath and tried blinking a few times to ease the transition.

When I was finally able to look around, I found myself in a small room. The blinding light was coming in from a tiny window. I turned away from it and spotted a wooden door and a gray-haired woman in a rocking chair holding a pile of cream-colored yarn.

She smiled at me. "There you are. I was hoping you would wake soon. How are you feeling, my dear?"

Terrible, horrible, wretched, I thought. "Not too bad," I rasped, unsure of what I should say; or what was going on; or where I was.

She smiled, "Not bad? My goodness, with all you have been through I would have thought you would say dreadful."

"Dreadful then," I said quickly, my already sore muscles tensing.

She laughed lightly and stuffed her knitting into her enormous apron pocket. "My name is Wendy. I am the innkeeper's wife here at The Old Wheel Inn in Avern. We've been looking after you since yesterday. May I have your name, My Lady?" she asked as she stood and gently checked the bandage on my head. Her hands felt cool against my skin, but her touch made the banging start again.

I automatically opened my mouth to reply, but no words came to my mind. She had asked me what felt like a normal question, however I had nothing to say. *My name ... did I even have such a thing?* I thought through the pounding in my head. I wasn't sure if I had one. I thought for a moment but couldn't come up with any sort of name. My brain was full of dark sludge, that wouldn't move away.

"I ... um ... I don't know if I have one," I finally admitted, my pulse beating quickly through my veins making the pain increase again.

"Of course, you do, sweet. It's all right to tell me. I promise you are safe here; those awful men will not harm you. We have an understanding with the outlaws. They leave us alone, and we serve them their ale," she laughed. "It is a priceless arrangement that we rely on. Believe you me. Besides the patrol chased them all off. You are safe here, My Lady."

She didn't seem to understand. I took a slow deep breath to try and calm my racing heart. I searched my mind again, but still nothing but sludge. I looked up at her and sniffed, sudden tears filling my eyes. "I should know what it is, shouldn't I?"

Wendy's eyebrows rose. Her smile faltered for a moment. "Yes, My Lady, I do believe you should. But it's all right; you will be feeling better soon. I am sure it will come to you." She patted my shoulder and turned to the door, "I'll go get you some soup." She smiled as she left, but I found little comfort in it.

What had happened to me? What did she mean "awful men"? I looked around the room, but my head began to pound again with enough force that I had to close my eyes. My wrist throbbed as much as my head did, but I was honestly sore all over. *What happened?* I thought again.

Wendy returned a few minutes later with a large man. He had a kind smile so I tried to not be afraid. I drew my covers up to my chin, however. It wasn't much of a shield but it was at least something.

"Hello, little lady. I am Charles the innkeeper. Finally come around, have you? You had quite a night, little lady." He chuckled to himself. "I couldn't believe me own eyes when I saw you roll off that cliff into the river."

I narrowed my eyes. *Into the river?*

I could feel the confusion on my face. He must have seen it, too. He looked over at Wendy who nodded. He dragged a rickety looking stool a little too close for my liking. Charles settled into it as if he were a professional storyteller.

"I was outside whistling me tune and taking care of a guest's horse, our stable is right next to the river, don't you know. When I heard the shouts and the squeal of an injured horse echoing in the evening air.

I looked up to see if I could find the poor beast and give a yelling to whomever it was hurt 'im. But I saw a girl instead. You were across the river with Manic's black-cloaked men surrounding you.

It gave me a terrible fright. I almost ran inside to save me own hide. I was positive I was about to witness one of their terrible murders, but instead witnessed a miracle. You, a Lady, dove into the river." He laughed again, slapped his leg and shook his head.

"It was amazing! Complete chaos broke out after that. The patrols came galloping down the hill and Manic's cowardly men scattered. They didn't even look back to see what became of you. Must of thought the river would do you in. I jumped in after you during the commotion. When I pulled you out, I was certain that you were lost, but then you started breathing. It was the best thing I'd ever seen, though Manic best never hear of it for your sake." He chuckled lightly and his eyes glazed as if he was reimagining the whole thing again. A huge smile grew wide on his face.

"I jumped into a river?"

"Yes, don't you remember?" he said, his huge smile faltering a bit.

"No."

His smile faded completely and he let out a moan. "Wendy said she thought your memories weren't good. But I was positive: last night would be something no one could forget, not ever."

I felt myself pale, and Charles forced a slight smile back onto his face. "Not to worry, little lady, I am sure it be coming back to you, soon."

"Yes, maybe it will help when the Prince arrives," said Wendy.

"The P-p-rince?" I stuttered.

The innkeeper and his wife, exchanged looks again. "Begging your pardon, My Lady, but I took your wet clothes to the wash and felt a crumple. So, I looked in your apron pocket and found your letter addressed to your friend, His Highness, The Royal Prince. It was hard to read; the river ruined most of it. We sent for him. We hope you don't mind, but we weren't sure what else to do."

Wendy dug into her apron and extracted a small crumpled square from her yarn. "I am sorry we opened it, My Lady, but we had no other choice."

I forced a feeble smile to my lips, and Wendy seemed satisfied. She helped me sit up so I could eat, and they both left the room.

After they left, I carefully unfolded the letter and read what I could of it. None of it seemed familiar. I stared at the signature at the end. Lady A? My name was a single letter? How absurd. Maybe the rest of it was washed out like half of the letter. I sighed. I guess Lady A would have to do for now. I set the letter aside, even more unsure than I was before.

I stared at the colorful vegetables swimming in the dark liquid, and tried to remember something, anything, before this room. I couldn't. Sighing and unsure of what else to do, I took a spoonful of soup and began to eat.

After the soup was gone, I leaned back against the coarse pillow and closed my eyes.

I must have fallen asleep because sometime later voices outside my door startled me awake. I stifled a moan as the pain shot through me anew. I held still until the pain lessened.

"Before you go in, I feel I must warn you, Your Highness— her injuries from the whole ordeal are extensive, and I'm afraid she is having trouble with her memory," Wendy's voice said.

"What do you mean?" asked another voice—a man's I did not know.

"She doesn't seem to remember anything at all. Not who she is, let alone my husband pulling her out of the river last night. I am sure it is only temporary. She did go through quite an ordeal."

"I see, thank you. You and your husband will be greatly rewarded for all you have done."

"We thank you, Your Highness."

I heard footsteps moving away, and I felt my pulse quicken again. I tried to pull my eyes away from the wooden door, but my head was not obeying my silent commands.

"James," said yet another man's voice. "How do you know this isn't some trick of Manic's. You have never met Lady A before, this could be anyone. This could be a ruse, a ploy, to trap you. Manic could have set this whole thing up."

"I understand your concern, Richard, but what if it is her? I can't leave her here alone and injured."

"How will you know, James? If she has no memories, how could you possibly know? How could you even test her?"

"The family portrait."

"What?"

"I saw her in the family portrait in her house."

"That's not enough, James."

"I appreciate your concern, Richard, and I will take it into consideration."

"Make sure you do, Sire."

"Why do you say that as if you are scolding me?"

"Because you think you are about to meet the one lady you have been dying to meet for over a year. I want to make sure you are on your guard."

"I am."

"Then forgive my tone, Sire."

A soft knock sounded on the door and I pulled the covers up to my chin. I tried to tell my racing heart to calm down. I wasn't sure what to do. I wanted to hide as much as I wanted answers. According to the letter, the Prince was my friend, but if he hadn't met me before how could that be true? I was so confused.

They knocked again and so I did the only thing that I could think of. "Come in," I trembled.

Chapter 4

~Lady A~

A young, well-dressed man stepped into my room and smiled. My heart stopped beating for a moment and the pain faded into the background, as I stared into his light blue eyes. His slightly wavy hair looked like melted chocolate someone had swirled with their finger. His soft curls brushed the tips of his ears. I strangely wanted to reach out and touch his hair.

A big man dressed the same as the first followed him inside the room. He had a blank expression on his slightly lined face as he closed the door and stood by it, feet apart and arms folded. I saw his silver sword glistening in a dark blue scabbard at his side and had to swallow a few times.

The younger man stood just inside the door and stared at me for a moment. The click of the door being closed seemed to break his concentration and he nodded to the stool that Charles had sat in earlier, "May I?"

Unsure, but curious, I nodded. He didn't act like a danger to me—at least not right now.

"Hello, Lady A, my name is Prince James," he said as he slowly walked to the chair. As he got closer my pulse quickened even more. The throbbing beneath my bandaged wrist worsened.

"Hello," I barely breathed. My lips started to quiver so I pressed them tightly together.

"Don't be afraid," he said, a sadness filling his eyes as he slowly sat on the stool. "I am a friend. I am here to help."

"Are you?" I said looking him over from his fancy clothes, covered by polished chainmail, to his shiny sword.

"Yes," he hung his head. "Lady A, I am so sorry. You should have never been hurt. Dan would be so angry. You do remember Dan, right?"

Tears came to my eyes, and I could not stop them. "I'm sorry, no."

He smiled, but I was positive he had forced it. He said he was a friend, but how did I know that? They were afraid I could be some sort of trap for him, but what about the other way around. What if he was working for the man Manic, who apparently wanted me dead?

"I am going to take you out of here to the castle in Saris. My healer is the best in the country and she will know how to help you recover. Will you allow that?"

I wanted to be fine with that decision, but I wasn't. How could I be? At the mention of the castle a shudder crawled down my arms making me shiver. *Was that a warning?* A sign that I shouldn't go anywhere with this man? I didn't know what was going on or whom I could trust.

"I don't think that I should," I said pulling the covers up to hide my trembling lips.

"Why not?" he asked looking like I had offended him.

I swallowed the slight guilt that I felt at his hurt expression and answered him. "How do I know you are not one of the evil men who did this to me?"

"She has a point," laughed the man at the door.

"Not helping, Richard," James said.

He let out a slow breath and looked me directly in the eye. "I assure you, My Lady, that I am not one of those outlaws. I am Prince James. More than that I am a knight of the realm. I have sworn an oath to follow the rules of chivalry. I am your friend. I am your brother's best friend. You can trust me. And Richard, back there by the door, I trust with my life every day."

I wanted to believe him. I could see sincerity in his light blue eyes, but sincerity could be faked—couldn't it? "Prove it," I whispered.

His eyebrows shot up, "Gladly, but how?"

I had no idea. I wanted to trust what he said; I truly did. I wanted to feel like I had some sort of an answer, some sort of real truth to hold on to. The Prince's friend sounded like a nice start, if it was true. An image of being tossed back into the rushing river filled my mind, and I quivered. I looked around for some kind of hint and spotted the crumpled letter. It was the only clue I had.

"Tell me, why did I have a letter addressed to you in my apron pocket?"

He smirked and leaned back in his chair looking at ease. I felt my heart beat speed up for a different reason. "Because you and I have been writing to each other for two years. I wrote to you yesterday, and you must have written a reply."

"And why did I tell you," I said pulling out the crumpled letter and unfolding it, "That Angelique was wrong?"

He laughed and Richard even had to stifle a chuckle. I didn't see how that question was funny at all. He leaned a little closer. "Because you, My Lady, are a tease. You and your brother won't tell me your name and think it is magnificent fun to watch me guess."

"So, you don't know my name either?" I asked. For some reason not being the only one who didn't know my name made me feel a little better. It shouldn't have, but it did.

"No, I don't, but that doesn't make me any less of a friend."

I looked over at Richard leaning against the door and his face softened a bit. I took that as a sign of approval or encouragement. It was a positive thing at least.

"I know you are scared, Lady A. I give you my word of honor as a knight, a gentleman, and a prince. I will not let any harm come to you. I only want to help."

I felt a flicker of warmth ignite in my heart and found myself nodding.

James's smile widened in approval. He stood. "I will send for the carriage immediately. We will go down to wait and let you rest, My Lady." He inclined his head toward me in a bow of respect. His hand lifted a bit as if he had wanted to grasp my hand or something, but he curled his fingers into his hand and pulled back.

I watched as they left and pulled the covers down from my face after the door closed. I still wasn't sure if I truly trusted him, but I had to trust someone to help me. I didn't want to stay at this inn forever. I honestly wanted to believe everything he said. Besides, his smile alone made me feel breathless.

Chapter 5

~James~

"So?" I asked Richard the moment after he closed the door behind us.

"She is indeed your Lady A; I am sure of it. But what did *you* think, James?"

I turned and walked down the hall to the rickety, wooden stairs. "I think she is beautiful." She really was, even though all I could see of her was her head covered in bandages. But those blue grey eyes of hers had captured me. "And I'm glad that at least she doesn't hate me."

Richard laughed and slapped me on the back. "Funny how that was your biggest worry only yesterday."

"Right, but definitely not today."

We found my other friends eating at a table downstairs in the noisy inn's main room.

"Is it her?" asked Roland before we even had a chance to sit down.

I nodded and dropped into a chair.

"Then why the long face?" asked Edgar. "She doesn't like you after all?"

"Who would, smelling like he does?" laughed Darwin.

I looked at Richard and let out a slow breath. "No, she doesn't remember me or anything at all. It seems that she was badly injured when she escaped Manic's men yesterday. She has a head injury that has caused her to forget everything."

"Even what …" started Roland, but he paused and looked around the room before lowering his voice. "What we came to talk to her and Dan about?"

"I'm afraid so. My Father is going to be livid or even more likely disappointed—not that he ever liked this crazy plan to begin with."

"It is only temporary right?" inquired Frederick. "She will regain her memories?"

"Let's hope so," I said not really wanting to discuss it further. "Darwin, I need you to ride to the castle and bring back a carriage."

"Yes, Sire," he said pushing his bowl aside and leaving directly. That's one reason why I liked him. He wasn't one to dawdle.

"Roland, Frederick, and Edgar please check Avern for any sign of Manic's men. I don't want to be surprised. If they have any inkling that she is alive they won't stop until they change that."

My friends bowed and left on their various tasks. I watched my men leave and put my head in my hands. Richard asked for two dinners to be brought over. I doubted I could eat. My mind was stuck on Lady A: the look of terror on her face, the bandages on her head and her arms haunted me. And what of Dan? If this is how she had fared, I could hardly bring myself to think about what might have happened to him.

A steaming bowl of stew was set before me by Wendy. She gave me a sad smile; I knew her thoughts were with Lady A as well. I reached for my spoon, but before I could take a bite something caught my eye that made me pause.

A tall man wearing a badly patched up, brown cloak had entered the bustling Inn. He stood for a moment his eyes searching the room. When he moved his hand to place a gold coin on the innkeepers counter, I saw a black cloak under the dingy one. I took a slow bite of stew as the man's eyes darted around the room again. He leaned in and whispered something to Charles.

The innkeeper tightened his jaw, smacked his offered coin off of the counter, and pointed to the door. I reached for my sword as the cloaked man turned toward the door, but before I could breathe, he took off running for the rickety stairs.

"Richard!" I shouted as I jumped up and chased after the man.

The man didn't look back as he raced up the stairs and down the upper hall. Wendy backed out of the door to Lady A's room, carrying a tray, and didn't see us coming. The cloaked man grabbed her and threw her backwards. I caught her before she hit the floor and was able to steady us both, but the man was already closing Lady A's door.

Richard raced past us with a look on his face that only a mother bear should have and pushed the door open. He threw the man to the floor, and knocked the dagger out of his hand.

"Stay back," I told Wendy as I darted inside the room. I looked away from the scuffling to see Lady A disappear under her covers. A grunt of pain pulled my attention back to the floor in time to see Richard holding his side and the traitorous scum scrambling to his feet.

"Halt!" I shouted as the traitor escaped to the other side of the room. He glanced toward Lady A, but he continued to the window, pausing only long enough to push the shutters open.

"Richard, take care of her," I shouted as I followed the man out onto the thatched rooftop of the lower level.

"You are one of them aren't you," I said as we crawled, the roof cracking with our every step.

He hooted, "You mean, one of those who be true to the real King of Salvina."

"No, you are a traitor, a pawn in a mad man's scheme, unless you are Manic himself?" The man paused at the edge of the rooftop and looked back my way.

"I'm not me master!" He smiled at me showing half-rotted teeth. The assassin looked down at the ground. I followed his gaze and saw a large pile of hay leaning against the wall of the inn.

He can't be serious? I thought.

"If I be him, you'd all be dead," laughed the man as he jumped into the pile of hay. I followed him, and before he could regain his footing pinned him to the ground. He struggled, but I held fast.

"What are you doing here?" I demanded.

"Taking care of some unfinished business," he grumbled.

"Which was?"

He laughed and spat in my face. "An irritant that must be dealt with."

"How dare you say such a thing about her!"

"Prince James," yelled Frederick as he rode into the yard. He directed his horse toward us and jumped off pulling rope out of his saddlebag as he came. He raced over and helped me tie up the traitor.

"Take him to the front of the inn and don't let him out of your sight," I demanded. "He seems to be in a talking mood. We might finally get a good description of his master if not more details of his plan."

"I will never betray him," growled the man.

"I doubt that," said Frederick as he tightened the ropes around the man's hands.

"Are you alright, James?" asked Frederick as he yanked the man to his feet.

"Yes, Fred," I said as I brushed hay off of my cloak.

He shrugged. "Move it you traitorous swill," he said to Manic's man. "You have an appointment with our dungeon that I would hate for you to miss." He gave the man a small push and made him walk to the front of the inn.

I looked up at the rooftop to see Richard's face watching us from the window. Lady A must be in hysterics. At least any of the other noble women I knew would be.

I raced back upstairs. I paused in the doorway when I heard that she and Richard were talking.

"We caught him, My Lady. There is no more danger."

"But there could be again?"

"I'm afraid so, My Lady. Manic isn't one to leave a job undone. They will try again."

"And that is why you all want me to go to the castle?"

"There is that, but Madge is known for her healing skills and we want you to get better. We swear to keep you safe, isn't that right, James?"

She turned her dazzling blue-grey eyes to me, and I couldn't help the smile that appeared on my lips. "It is," I said.

She let out a slow breath and nodded, "I will try to trust you."

"That's enough for now," I said.

It would have to be.

Chapter 6

~Lady A~

I tried not to groan when Wendy came in a little while later to help me get into my ragged and torn dress. The pain intensified with every movement, but I gritted my teeth and worked through it. I wasn't going to go anywhere without being properly dressed. As Wendy changed the bandage on my head, I found myself braiding the ends of my long hair.

"Would you like me to braid your hair, My Lady?" she asked as she finished with the bandage.

"No, thank you, I don't want to disturb the bandage," I said letting my hair go.

She nodded and offered me her arm. I gasped as I stood. We waited for a moment until the pain started to fade, and tried again. I took a step and found that my legs refused to hold my weight. I attempted another step, but nearly fell. Wendy steadied me and helped me sit back down.

"Oh dear," Wendy giggled clearly trying to lighten the mood. "I think we will have to have someone stronger than I to help you out."

She went to the door, whispered something to whoever was out there, and came back in. "I wish you well, My Lady. I hope your memories return soon and that the cloaked men never find you. And if you find yourself passing through Avern again remember you will always have a room here."

"Thank you, Wendy, for everything."

"Of course," she said as a knock sounded on the door.

I sucked in my breath as Prince James entered the room. Some how I knew it would be him. How I could be a friend with someone as handsome as the prince, I had no idea. But he was convinced it was true, and I had to trust that. It was all I had. Why else would he risk his life for mine? I tried to smile, but I am sure it looked more like a grimace.

"I have come to escort the lady to her carriage," he said with an over exaggerated bow.

"Why, thank you, good sir," I said with a true smile tugging at my lips.

His smile faded from his lips, which was not the reaction I had expected. *Did I say something wrong?*

"Where did you get that?' he said touching the fabric of the blue cloak Wendy had fastened around me?

"I don't know?" I said. "Wendy brought it in with my clothes. It's the same as yours," I said looking between the two cloaks. "Am I not supposed to have it?" I asked reaching for the silver clasp.

"Actually, I am fairly certain that you are," he said. "Dan must have given it to you."

I looked at the cloak again. It was a little big for me. I suppose he had to be right.

"May I?" he said, as he reached down for me. I nodded. He scooped me up into his arms as if I weighed nothing more than a summer blanket. My head throbbed harder with the movement, and I sucked in a sharp breath. Before I realized what I was doing, I let my head fall on his shoulder.

"Sorry," I breathed as I tried to move, but found it impossible.

"You're fine," he said. "I will try to be gentle."

He carried me down the stairs and out into the light of the evening sun. I opened my eyes when I felt the air hit my face. It felt nice after the stuffy little room. Four soldiers bowed to us as we approached a red and gold trimmed carriage.

"Lady A, I'd like you to meet my friends and most trusted men: Edgar, Darwin, Frederick, and Roland."

"Hello," I said automatically, but my eyes were drawn to the black-cloaked man who was tied to the back of the carriage. His eyes were dark and he bared his rotten teeth at me as if he were a vicious dog. If I had been closer, I am sure he would have tried to bite me.

"Don't worry about him, Lady A. He's going to be interrogated and then locked up for a very long time," James said moving past the man.

I tried not to worry about him as Prince James placed me on the soft cushions in the carriage, but the cloaked man's menacing look would not leave my mind. Dark sludge and the image of that face filled my every thought. Richard climbed in with us and sat across from the Prince. He gave me an encouraging smile as the carriage began to move.

The slight swaying movements made my head begin to pound again. "I think I will close my eyes for a while," I said as I buried my head into the seat. The men were silent at first but soon began to talk about patrols. I must have fallen asleep because I jerked awake when the carriage quickly slowed to a stop and loud shouting penetrated the carriage.

Edgar rode up to the window, "James, he escaped."

"What do you mean, escaped?" James said turning to look out the window.

"Somehow he got out of his bonds." James put his hand on his sword and swung open the door.

Roland rode up as James stepped out. "He wrangled his way out of the ropes and darted off into the woods."

"Then what are you two doing here?" James shouted looking at both Edgar and Roland.

"Frederick and Darwin chased after him," said Edgar.

"Both of you get after them. We cannot lose him."

"Yes, Sire," they replied as they turned and rode off.

"James do you want me..." started Richard.

"No, we need to get Lady A to Saris. Drive on." James shouted as he climbed back inside. "After we arrive, if we have not heard good news then I want you to return with reinforcements."

Richard nodded and sat back. James was shaking his head and mumbling to himself. The easiness that had been in the carriage was gone. I wasn't sure if I should feel scared. I knew I didn't want the evil looking man near me so I was honestly a little relieved. Besides, I was going to the castle where I would be safe, but a small part of me knew that the man returning to his master wasn't a good thing for me. Not at all.

A little while later we rode through the gates of Saris the capital city. The town was bustling as they closed down the market for the day, but everyone moved out of the way of the royal carriage. It wasn't much longer before we rode through the gates to the castle. James and Richard both looked a little anxious as we pulled up to the castle entrance, and I felt my own heart speed up a bit.

James glanced over at Richard who nodded, seeming to understand James's unspoken command. He stepped out of the carriage and rushed away.

"Lady A?" asked James. "Will you allow me to carry you once again?"

"Yes, thank you." I wasn't willing to embarrass myself by falling down the castle stairs at the moment.

He lifted me up, and I hoped that he didn't mind my head on his shoulder again. He seemed not to for which I was grateful.

The castle torches were all lit making the white stones glow orange and shimmer as if washed with gold. Prince James carried me up the steps and through the doors into the entrance Hall.

A shriek caused me to look around. I found a young girl in a flowing pink dress and bouncy brown curls bounding down the stairs.

"Oh, Lady A, we were so worried. Mother and I have been pacing most of the afternoon, and I have been plastered to the windows for the last half hour looking for you. What a terrible thing to have happened—being attacked! Were you terrified? Did you faint? I would have fainted, I am sure."

"Iree …" James tried to interrupt.

"I guess I might not have fainted, maybe I would have had a heart attack or something else. Oh, your poor head. Is that dried blood? Darwin didn't tell us much but he is not that talkative anyway."

"Iree, she doesn't need your endless chatter right now. Please ignore my twelve-year-old sister."

"James, how could you say such a thing? I can talk to her if I want," said Iree sticking out her lower lip.

"Iree, enough," said a strong, female voice. I looked away from Iree to see an exquisite lady with a gold crown woven in her dark hair descending the stairs. "Hello, Lady A, I am Queen Alexia. We have a room prepared for you on the second floor."

"Thank you, Mother," the Prince said as he turned toward the large staircase.

"James, in here first," called another voice, but this one had a sharp tone to it. James groaned, but only loud enough for me to hear him. He turned and carried me into the room where the voice had come from.

"Father, I swear I can…" started James.

"You are not going to tell me that you can explain, are you?" said the stern-faced man that looked like a more chiseled version of James. The bit of grey in his hair, only added to the strictness of his gaze.

"No, father, it was inexcusable for us to lose a prisoner," said James as he gently set me down on a chair.

"No, it was more than inexcusable. It was foolish." The king turned stony eyes toward me. "I have half a mind to think she's a part of it."

"What? Not a chance," James said standing in front of me like a shield.

The Kings eyes narrowed as he craned his head to look closer at me. He took in my haggard looking appearance, his frown deepening. "She could be a fake, a plant. I would not put it past Manic to pull a stunt like that to infiltrate the castle. No one would suspect her. Except me."

"She is not a fake, father."

"You don't know that!"

"Good heavens," said the Queen from the door. She glared at her husband as she strode into the room. "We haven't lost our good sense and honor to this bully, have we? I will not have us blaming innocent girls because someone is getting short tempered."

The King turned his furious eyes toward his wife. "She could be anyone with this so-called amnesia, and there is no one who can vouch for her."

"No one except me? She looks almost exactly like her mother."

"That is not proof—"

"I think it is!" she said matching the Kings intense look.

The King threw his hands in the air and walked to his window simmering.

"The poor girl has been through enough without you interrogating her, William. We trust the Albons. This is uncalled for. Surely, you can see that."

The King's face was still hard when he turned to look our way. "Go."

"Come on, James—Lady A," said the queen as she opened the door.

James picked me back up and we all left silently. I looked back at the King. His arms were folded and his jaw was tight. He kept his eyes turned toward the window. He was clearly worried for his Kingdom. I wished I knew what to say to help, but there was nothing in my mind.

When we got back to the staircase, the Queen placed a hand on James' arm. "Any news about Sir Daniel?"

"Not yet I am afraid."

The Queen sighed, "I have been waiting to write to the Albons, I had hoped for some better news but it seems I have no choice now."

"Who are the Albons?' I asked not liking feeling completely lost.

The Queen's eyebrows rose, but she quickly smiled. "They are your parents, dear."

"Oh."

"I wish they were in Loth or even Tefton. It will take two weeks for the letter to even arrive in Uree," the queen mumbled as she walked next to us.

After another staircase, we turned down a long hallway lined with suits of armor. Near the end of the hall she opened a door and a servant bowed as we entered a large beautiful room. Two women who smelled like an herb garden approached and bowed as James set me down on the bed. Iree came bounding in behind us and flopped on the bed beside me.

"I will stay with her James," she said rolling onto the end of the bed, her light pink dress poofing out all around her.

"Iree, she really doesn't need you bouncing about."

"Well, you can't stay in here because you are a boy," said Iree eying her brother.

"We will take care of her, son," said the Queen.

James's jaw tightened, but he nodded, bowed, and with one last look my way he left the room.

"James said she can't remember anything because of her head injury. Her right arm was badly injured as well," the Queen said addressing the two other women in the room. I watched as one began digging through her bags, while the other poured some water into a basin. I looked at Iree and she offered me a huge smile, her light brown curls bouncing around her rosy cheeks.

Don't be nervous, I told myself. *They are here to help.*

"Madge will have you feeling better in no time; she has the magic of healing. And Netta will be your personal servant while you are with us."

"Thank you … my Queen."

"Alexia, my dear."

I felt my eyes widen, but she laughed. "You might not remember much, but we all feel like we know you. Even if we haven't

60

met, at least as far as we can remember, but Iree and I never missed out on an opportunity to talk about you with James or Dan."

I gave her a weak smile. They were all very nice, but I still felt so lost.

"We are so glad to have you here, my dear. I'm sorry it has to be because of injury. I know that James and Dan never meant for you to get hurt. I want you to know that even if you can't remember anything else, know that they never meant for any of this to happen. And we will do all we can to help you regain your memories."

I felt tears prick at my eyes. "Thank you, that helps me feel better already."

Alexia gave my shoulder a squeeze. Madge arranged her supplies next to me and gently started prodding my injured hand.

"So, do you think you and James will ever get married?" Iree blurted out a moment later with a dreamy look in her eyes. My jaw fell open, and I am sure I resembled a dead fish perfectly.

"Iree!"

"What, I'm only curious," said Iree. "Rosetta is going to be so furious you're here." Iree laughed.

"Iree Isabella Katarina Monroe, if you are going to cause problems, I will make you leave," said the Queen.

Iree harrumphed, but her eyes remained bright. I wasn't sure why she had asked me if I would marry her brother. Did the Prince and I have an understanding? I didn't think so. He had said we were friends, not engaged. But then why would Iree say such a thing? And who was Rosetta? I wanted to ask my questions but with the healer unwrapping my bandages I knew now wasn't the time.

"Iree," I said trying not to whimper. "I am not able to remember anything before this afternoon. So right now, I quite doubt it."

"You can't remember anything?" she asked eyes wide. "Nothing at all?"

"No," I said as Madge the Healer began to lay dried leaves on my wound. She was murmuring under her breath as she did so. No one else was looking at her strangely so I decided this must be normal.

"Not even your name?" Iree asked a moment later with a mischievous look growing on her face.

"I'm afraid not. Everyone keeps calling me Lady A though."

Iree burst out laughing and nearly rolled off the bed onto the floor. The Queen's lips even twitched a bit.

"What is it?" I asked looking from one person to the other. "Did I miss something?"

"Yes," said Iree. "The best joke ever," she said, laughing hard once again. "Poor James."

A tiny flicker of a new memory ignited in my mind. "Wait, I know about this joke. The Prince said I have been teasing him."

"I'd say more like making him crazy," giggled Iree.

"Iree, honestly," said the Queen through her own smile.

"It's fine, Lady A," said Iree patting my shoulder. "I think he actually likes it."

I couldn't help it. A real smile crept up my face. I may not know much, but I was beginning to think I was going to like Princess Iree.

Chapter 7

~James~

My father was usually a patient king. He cared about his people and he tried to keep the peace between those who attempted to start wars. I knew if he was getting frustrated that his extraordinary amount of patience had been used up. Manic and his claims for the throne this year had pushed him to his limit more often than not lately. It'd been four days since we found Lady A, but I've had little to no luck in finding any sign of Manic or Dan. I was starting to understand how my father felt.

"What are our options, Son?" my father said loosening his collar as he paced behind the desk in his study.

"I don't see any new options father, just the same old ones. We have to continue on as we always have: trying to snare Manic, that is if he ever decides to stop acting like a coward and accompany his men. And we can hope in the meantime that Lady A will regain her memories, that one of his men will betray him, or that we will hear from Dan soon. That is all I can say."

He stopped his pacing, sat down behind his desk, and looked me right in the eye.

"The people cannot live in fear any longer. This has to stop, son. I am tired of Manic's claims to the throne. I don't care if he says his great-great grandfather Arnold was forced out by my great-great grandfather Albert. History is what it is. I will protect my kingdom from a bully like him and his sentences of death. Our good people will not follow him and his ridiculous false claims. I want this over with."

"I know, father. I am doing my best. You will be glad to hear that we have received word from our scouts that some of Manic's riders have been loitering about the city of Jude. I feel, as do they, that his men aren't there for some casual off-time. I think he's scouting his next target. As usual, I am sure he will say that Jude will either side with him or fall, but he doesn't seem ready to attack tomorrow.

It almost feels like he is waiting for something. This isn't like him to let his men be seen and not already be inflicting his horrors. I think something is different this time; I wish I knew what it was."

My father nodded. "Have the scouts keep us informed. I want you to choose your best men to lead the troops to Jude. We will take Manic's hesitation and use it to our advantage."

"But shouldn't we be worried about why he is going about this differently?"

"Honestly, son, I don't care if he is trying to pull something. He will expect us to watch and wait until he makes a move, like we have done in the past. This time we will get there first. This time we will apprehend him in our own surprise."

I stood. "I will inform Roland and Edgar to prepare to lead their men to Jude right away, father."

"Good."

"I assure you, if Manic is with them we will find him."

"See that you do."

He dismissed me with a wave of his hand and I left.

Hopefully, Manic was actually with his men, this time.

Far too often we have been able to prevent disaster and capture most of Manic's men, but as far as we knew he has never been with them. I wasn't sure if I should start thinking of him as smart instead of a coward. But one thing was for certain—he needed to be stopped—and soon.

Richard was waiting for me outside the door as usual.

"I assume he was unhappy with our report," he said before I opened my mouth.

"Of course, he was, but we knew that going in. He was somewhat pleased with our scout's discovery of Manic's men in Jude," I said as we walked down the hall toward my room.

"And Lady A?"

"He was disappointed that she still can't remember anything. Just as the rest of us are. He was nearly as angry as I am that we cannot find Dan."

"James, it is not your fault. You are doing everything you can."

"Yes, it is my fault, Richard. The one time that Lady A and I didn't agree on stopping Dan, and everything is falling apart. Dan and I had imagined his idea turning out so differently. Our whole plan has failed."

I paused and looked out the window at the setting sun as another day ended mocking my lack of accomplishment.

"Richard, I failed her, my father, my country. How could I have let myself do that?"

"James, you didn't ..."

"Don't, Richard. Don't try to convince me that things are all right. Nothing has gone right at all."

I fell onto the window seat and fingered my sword. Richard sat down beside me. He didn't speak, but from his expression I knew he was gathering his thoughts. I realized most princes wouldn't have sat there waiting for their bodyguard to figure out what to say to them. But Richard was more than a bodyguard—he was my friend, my constant companion, and confidant for as long as I can remember.

Finally, after a few minutes, and after my racing blood calmed down to a steadier pace, he spoke, "I know this wasn't how you imagined meeting her."

I let out a slow breath. As usual, he found the real reason for my frustration.

"Not at all," I groaned. "It must have been crazy for me to think so, but I was hoping when I finally got to see her, I'd feel like she was everything I'd imagined her to be."

"That she would be the one you wished to marry?"

I glared at him. If anyone but Richard had said that they would have been punished, and he knew it.

He smiled, "I know better than anyone how smitten you were with her. I know how much you wished to bring her back with you, and how you teased your mother and Iree about a fall wedding."

"Such crazy dreams seem unimportant right now, Richard."

"I know. It's the loss of those dreams that has me worried about you."

"But they aren't lost forever you know; we can fix this," I said though my tone wasn't as confident as I wished.

"I know, James, but if you are going to make things right for her you have to actually start talking to her. If you know her as well as you think then help her remember. She needs you, just as much as your country needs you."

I looked down at my boots. I hadn't been to see her since I'd dropped her off at her room when we arrived. I knew it was partly because I had been gone looking for Dan, but it was also because I didn't know what to say to her. What could I say?

'I'm sorry you were right.' She'd just look at me with that confused look in her eyes.

"I will after I get back," I said as I stood. "Roland, Edgar, and I have some place to be."

"Which means I do, too," he said.

"Too true, old man."

We walked in silence after that. My thoughts went immediately to Lady A. It was true I was foolishly in love with the girl with whom I exchanged letters. The question I didn't have an answer to was—Did I love the girl who had lost her memory?

Chapter 8

~Lady A~

Over the next few days, Iree, Madge, and Netta visited me multiple times a day. They were always offering herbs and healing magic for the pain, or daisies to brighten the room. The Queen came a few times as well but the Prince never came to visit. At first, I was worried I had been tricked and that he never was my friend. That maybe they were healing me only to torture me. I eventually realized it probably wasn't proper for him to come see me while I was healing in bed.

I would have still expected him to at least check up on me. Finally, I decided to stop tormenting myself and scrounged up the courage to ask Iree about him.

"He's been gone a lot. He's home only to sleep a little and then out again before the sun has risen."

"Why?"

She bit her lip. "I'm not sure what I am supposed to tell you. Am I allowed to mention Dan?"

"Sure," I said. I understood that Dan was my brother and that they were worried about him.

"Well, James has been out looking for him. I guess he has no good leads and that doesn't make him happy at all, but mother says he got back a little while ago and will probably stay until we hear anything new. So that's good, right?" She smiled and hopped off the bed. "I have to go to dance lessons now." She rolled her eyes, and twirled out of the room.

That afternoon, Madge suggested I try taking a walk outside. I had taken a few turns about my room, but I hadn't ventured out yet. I was more than ready to do so. I wasn't about to let my sore legs deter me. Netta guessed it was from riding a horse. None of us really knew for sure.

I was relieved to be brought a real dress. It was a soft blue with darker blue embroidery. The sleeves were loose and opened wide at my elbow which I appreciated because of my wrapped wrist. Netta and Madge guessed my arm would take the longest to feel like new again even with their magic. Thankfully, my other injuries were healing quickly.

A servant was called to be my escort along with my own personal bodyguard, Egan. He looked to be only about my same age, but that might have been because of his white blond hair and baby face. They wanted people to be with me in case I got too tired to return on my own.

The old man servant inclined his head when he arrived but kept his eyes on his grimy-looking hands. He was an old man and honestly, I was afraid Egan and I would have to carry him back. Iree was busy with her mother and Netta claimed she wasn't the best choice of companions in my present state of health. I was unwilling to argue with her and lose my chance to be free of that one room, so I took my chances with the old man servant.

The moment we walked outside; I felt my muscles relax more than they had in days. I breathed in the air that hit us and turned my face into the wind to catch more of the movement. It was heavenly.

Egan and the old servant didn't say anything as we walked. Egan kept looking around. I had to stifle a snort, he reminded me of a chicken searching for food. I assumed he had to make certain we were not about to be attacked.

The old servant only picked black things out of his fingernails, and grunted if I said anything to him. I was beginning to think that the fresh air wasn't worth it for all the company these two were not providing when I spotted the prince and Iree. Knowing that the servant would just totter along beside me with Egan at our heels, I approached a large yellow rose bush. I bent down and peered through the leaves. It wasn't spying, not really.

"James, why don't you go and visit her now that you are back?"

"I will soon, Iree."

Iree's hands moved to her hips and her lips formed a thin line. "Don't you like her anymore?"

"I still like her a lot, but she doesn't even remember anything about me. And I was hoping to return with Dan. I was counting on him to know how to help her. But I can't find him."

"Do you think he is still with the bad man?" asked Iree laying a comforting hand on her brothers' arm.

"Yes, that is what I am hoping: that he is still undercover and hasn't had a chance to let us know what is going on."

"Don't worry, James, you will find him," Iree said in her usual happy manner. "Now how about you come with me to visit Lady A? Maybe something you say will help her memories to come back. Madge said she needs a trigger or something like that."

"And you think I could help with that?"

"Yes!"

"Of course, you do," he said tickling his little sister. She squealed and raced away right toward my hiding place. Her eyes brightened when she saw my face through the roses. I was caught.

"Lady A, you're up," she squealed racing around the bush. She nearly knocked me over with her hug. James reached out and steadied me.

"Be careful, Iree," he scolded.

"Whoops, sorry. I am so glad to see you walking about," she said smiling brightly at me again, her eyes darting between her brother and I.

"I am, too," I said. My eyes strayed from her in favor of her brother.

He was watching me, too. As our eyes connected, for a moment, it felt like the world around us faded out until only he and I stood in detail.

Iree giggled and started backing away bringing back the world and herself, "Oh … oh dear, I forgot mother had something important for me to do. I should go." She squeezed my hand and took off waving as she went. But it was a ruse. Only a moment later I watched her back track to some red rose bushes in a failed attempt at spying.

The prince shook his head at his sister's silliness and offered me his arm. "May I?"

"Thank you."

The servant who had continued his nail picking turned and left at a nod from the Prince. My bodyguard backed away a few paces keeping his watchful eyes on our surroundings. My stomach felt like it jumped up and down when I took James's offered arm.

This is what I have been waiting for, I thought.

I shook my head. Why did I think that? The excitement that coursed through me didn't make sense. I had only taken his arm.

He led me across the garden to a wooden bench.

"If it is okay with you, Your Highness, I would rather walk," I said.

"Are you sure?"

"Yes, please. I have been forced to stay still for far too long."

He nodded and we continued slowly walking through the rose gardens. I couldn't enjoy the roses or contoured bushes like I had before. Now that I was with the Prince, I was bursting with questions. I looked at him out of the corner of my eye but he kept his eyes facing forward. Unwilling to be tortured by the unknown anymore I cleared my throat.

"Prince James, do you think my brother Dan could be … injured also?"

He smiled sadly, nodded his head, and looked away from me. "Unfortunately, yes, I do. He could very well be hurt or worse." He didn't say anything more, but I could tell there was something more he wanted to say.

"Prince James, what is it?" I said pulling him to a stop.

"Nothing. Don't worry about it," he said looking me directly in the eye. I felt a warm tremor move up my arms. "And please, Lady A, call me James."

"Thank you, it would be an honor," I said pulling my eyes away from his.

We continued walking down the path in silence. I was positive I should have been dignified and taciturn and at least pretend to be satisfied with his answer, but I couldn't help it. I could not accept "nothing" for an answer. I turned and stepped in front of him so that he had to look at me.

"I don't need any more mystery in my life Prince James. You claim to be a friend of mine. So please don't hide anything from me. No one else will tell me anything. If you truly are my friend then don't keep things from me. Especially not now."

He took a deep breath and ran a hand through his hair; making his soft curls stand out at odd angles. "You warned us, Lady A. You told Dan and I not to do this. You begged me to lock Dan in the dungeons when he told you about our crazy idea to capture Manic. But I refused. And now you are injured," he said looking at the new bandage wrapped around my head. "And Dan is missing."

I sighed. I had hoped his answer would make me feel less anxious, but it didn't. "James, I wish I knew what you were talking about. Or why I should be afraid. Who is this Manic creature?"

He snickered and we began walking again, "It's probably a good thing you don't remember."

"No, it is not, James," I said tugging him to a stop. "I need to remember. It could be the very thing to get my head out of the dark clouds that seem to fill it. I can take it. Please, I need to know."

He studied me for a moment. "A creature, as you called him is close. He is more like a monster, a monster that plunders, burns villages, and murders people as he goes. It is all in his hope to take over the kingdom to which he feels he is the rightful ruler. You should be afraid because Manic wants you dead. He nearly accomplished that goal once and I know he will try again. If Manic wants you dead—" James raised his eyes to mine and reached for my hand. "He will stop at nothing until you are."

A small shiver prickled my arms. I kept my chin up and my face as expressionless as I could, but I couldn't stop my eyes from widening. I hoped I hid most of my reaction to what he said because now that I had him talking, I didn't want him to stop.

"But why would any of this involve me? As a knight I can understand why my brother would be a part of it all, but how did I get mixed up in it?"

He looked around and steered me to a bench by a large Maple tree. We sat and he wrung his hands. "I want you to know that your brother is my best knight. My best friend. I would go into any battle without a moment's consideration with him fighting at my side. Dan is also reckless. You and I spent the last two years trying to cure him of attempting his crazy schemes.

But one night when he was on guard duty at the castle gates, we stayed up all night hashing out ideas of how to stop Manic and his riders for good. We finally came up with the plan for Dan to turn spy. It was the only way we could think of to learn what Manic was planning."

"You don't know?"

"We know he wants the throne. We know he is willing to destroy the kingdom on his way to do it. But his tactics are random. He is either threatening our people in the streets to join him and get to know whom the true king should be, or he is burning down villages. We have stopped many of his plans, but he is never with his men when we do. He has a bigger plan than what he has done so far. He has told us as much, but what it is we still don't know. That is what Dan was attempting to find out."

"I see. I was against this plan?"

He smirked. "More than that. You were so angry with us. But eventually you realized that there would be no talking us out of our plan and you accepted your job as Dan's report person. It was too dangerous for him to come to me while he was trying to convince Manic, he was a traitor."

"Oh no, now you can't find Dan, and I've lost my memory."

He nodded.

"James, I probably knew enough to find Dan," I said looking up at him. I expected to see anger in his eyes, but the opposite was true.

"No, you knew enough to expose Manic to bring him down. You knew his plan. I was on my way to your house that night to get Dan's report because your letters told me that you both knew everything, we needed to know to stop Manic."

I felt my heart start to crumble and I pulled my hand out of his. I walked a pace away trying to force the trembling out of my throat. "James, I'm so ..."

"Don't you say it, Lady A," he said jumping up and turning me around to face him. "You do not need to apologize for any of this. This is not your fault. This is mine. If anyone is to apologize it should be me." He crouched down in front of me and took my good hand in his. "I am so sorry. I hope you can find a way to forgive me."

His eyes found mine and I felt my cheeks grow warm as I stared into his light blue eyes. "I forgive you, James." He slowly raised my hand to his lips and pressed a soft kiss to my fingers.

"James, we can still fix this." I said. He shook his head. "No, listen. Madge and Netta have been looking through any magical or herb book they can find, and they said my memory might be able to come back if we can find the right trigger."

"So Iree told me," he said still looking at my hand in his. I thought about pulling it away from him but I found I didn't want to.

"James, if I can get my memories back then I can remember what Dan told me. We could still bring Manic down and rescue Dan. Maybe this crazy plan won't be for naught." He was nodding, but still didn't look at me. I reached for his other hand and he let me take it. "James, will you please help me?"

He was silent for a moment, "Of course I will, but shouldn't we wait until you are better?"

"No, I am healing fine, faster than I thought was possible. And honestly I'd like to remember more than the last few days."

He chuckled, "Well let's get started. What do we need to do?" he asked, his eyes brightening a bit more.

"Madge said I need to be exposed to different things. Anything that could be familiar to me. The trick is that the trigger could be anything, but it has to be the right thing."

He smiled fully and stood. "Well Lady A, what do you say we get your memories back?"

"I thought you would never ask," I said smiling brighter than I had in days.

Chapter 9

~Lady A~

Iree came bounding into my room the next morning and flopped onto the bed. "Lady A?"

"Good Morning, Iree," I said from behind the dressing curtain. Netta was helping to lace me into my dress. Iree poked her head around the side of the partition, her light brown curls bouncing off in odd angles.

"I have the most splendid plan, Lady A," she giggled rolling onto her back and hugging herself. "I have the perfect idea of how to get your memories back—a tea party hosted by me. I have it all planned: Cook will make the white cake, and we will have strawberries, and the yummy tea, not that nasty stuff they make me drink when I am sick. You will come, won't you?"

I laughed, at the way her brows pinched in worry. "Of course, I will come."

She clapped her hands, her smile so wide a dimple appeared in her cheek. "Oh, thank you! I am so excited; this is my first tea that I have been allowed to plan all by myself. Oh no! We have to have blankets to sit on. I forgot that. See you this afternoon, Lady A. I have so much to do." With a squeal she rolled off the bed and bounced out of the room.

Netta and I both burst out laughing. "You know, dear, her idea isn't bad. I am sure you had tea parties before, it could very well be the thing."

"Well why not?" I said. "I am more than willing to give it a try."

That afternoon, escorted by James, I attended Iree's tea. She grinned and curtsied as low as she could go, as we approached, and with wide sweeping arms she showed us to the light pink, fluffy blanket she had placed under the shade of a large maple tree. "Welcome to my tea," she said slowly to match her arm movements.

James and I shared a glance. Both of us fought down a giggle. "Thank you," I said. James accompanied me to my spot on the blanket and swept his sister his finest bow, I was sure.

"Iree, this looks fantastic," he pulled out of his coat a bright red poppy and handed it to her. "For the hostess."

"Thank you," she said giving it a sniff. She set her flower by her plate making sure it was in the right spot and began pouring tea in the small light pink cups.

James sat down next to me and turned slowly to face me. "Don't you worry, Lady A, I haven't forgotten you," he whispered as he pulled a yellow flower from his jacket and handed it to me.

"Thank you," I said startled by his thoughtfulness. I took the flower and brought it to my nose. I couldn't help the smile that spread across my face as I stared at the deeper yellow center that looked like a star. I reached out and softly touched the heart-shaped petals. "I remember you," I murmured.

James smirked and reached over to give my hand a squeeze.

"I have this feeling that I love this flower," I whispered looking between him and the flower.

His smile widened, "It's a primrose and I know you do. You told me so yourself."

"Really?"

He nodded.

"I would like to welcome you both to my first, all planned by me, tea party. I hope you found your way here easily," Iree said raising her cup to her lips, her pinkie thrust out as straight as it would go. James and I stifled our laughter again as we nodded and took sips of our own, mimicking her movements.

"Excellent. I have white cake and strawberries for you both to enjoy." She uncovered each dish as she described each item. "Unless you don't like them, then don't eat them," she said taking a large bite out of a strawberry. We ate for a moment enjoying the calm breeze. After a few moments Iree leaned in really close to me, her bright blue eyes growing wider.

"Do you remember anything yet?"

I felt my smile falter. I wish I had a better answer for her.

"No, nothing other than I remember that I love primroses. James brought me one."

She frowned so quickly it was almost comical. "Well that is a tiny something. Are you sure you remember nothing else?"

I shook my head. "I'm sorry."

She sighed, deflating into an un-lady-like heap. "That's okay, Lady A."

I was trying to come up with something to cheer her up when her eyes suddenly brightened and she snapped her fingers. "Hey that's it. James we should try to guess her name. Maybe if we find the right one her memories will come back. Oh, let's try it please? I bet you have your list with you; you always have your list."

"List?" I asked looking at James.

He glared at Iree as she dove across her tea and reached into his coat pocket. Iree pulled out a ragged looking paper, held it out of James's reach and danced around. "This is the list of names that he has tried guessing so far. There are lots of them."

"James, what is going on?" I said studying the two of them.

"Remember how I told you that you have been teasing James?!" Iree giggled. "Every letter he guesses and every time he is wrong. It's such fun! It wasn't Annie," said Iree reading the paper she had taken from James. "Or Alice, or Alina or Rose ..."

"Iree, I think you are embarrassing one of your guests."

"Oh, dear," she said dropping the paper. "Please, forgive me, Lady A."

"I meant me!" he grumbled reaching for Iree again. She jumped back and held the paper over her head. Iree and I both ignored his disapproving look.

"Of course, I forgive you, Iree," I said as I snatched the paper from her before James could. Scrawled in a bold hand were a list of women's names, most of them started with A, but there were a few that started with other letters. "James, did you really guess all of these?"

"Yes. No one would tell me and I wanted to know. So, I kept guessing," he said playing with his napkin. A warmth entered my chest as I looked at him, a warmth that I wish I held with me all the time.

"James, Lady A, please let us guess," begged Iree.

James still wouldn't look up, so I nodded, and Iree let out a rather un-ladylike cheer.

"Oh, I know, it has to be Adorabella. No, no, no wait, Keturah."

I kept my eyes on James who wouldn't meet my eye, so I turned and grinned at Iree instead. "I guess not, Iree."

"Darn. Okay Megan, no Ava, how about Katherine?"

I shook my head.

"Come on, James, guess," giggled Iree.

He sighed, "Adalie?"

I shook my head. As much as I wanted them to, none of them resonated with me.

"Annabelle?"

"Abigail? Guinevere? Rebecca? Jenessa? No ... no I got it, Ariellna," said Iree before she stuffed a huge bite of cake into her mouth.

"No, I guess not," I said taking a sip of tea. "Are we doing this right, James?"

His eyebrows rose, and he finally looked up at me. He opened and closed his mouth a few times as if he was struggling for an answer.

"Excuse me," said Richard, approaching our tea party. He bowed to Iree who giggled at him. "May I borrow the Prince?"

Iree nodded, chewing another bite of cake. James inclined his head to both of us and walked a few paces away. He and Richard whispered for a few moments before James took off running. Richard offered us a smile and a bow before he darted off after the prince.

"What was that about?" I said watching their retreating forms.

Iree shrugged and kept eating. I took a bite of a strawberry, but my mind was on the prince. *Why had he taken off like that?* I wondered. I was having a hard time coming up with any ideas. My sluggish mind seemed to lack imagination. I was worried; however, he wouldn't have run off like that if it were anything good.

I looked at Iree who nodded to the cake. I put a piece on my plate. As I did, I spied James's crumpled napkin. It was interesting that I had been teasing him. *I must have some wit,* I thought. With that happy clue in mind I took a bite of cake, which made Iree smile brighter.

Chapter 10

~James~

Richard's timing had never been so perfect. I wasn't sure how I was going to explain Lady A's own game to her. I didn't fully understand her motivation; even though I did find it enjoyable. All I really knew was it was because of her game that she had caught my interest more than any other lady.

"Richard, thank you for saving me. You always seem to know the right moment to interrupt."

"James, we have news."

"What kind of news?"

Richard looked toward the tea party and lowered his voice. "Sir Daniel's horse, Narcissus, was discovered wandering around east of the Albon's property. He was just brought here a few minutes ago. The poor beast had an arrow in his rear."

I felt my jaw tighten. "What kind of arrow?"

"Black with red-tipped feathers."

I clenched my fists. "Anything else?"

"I don't know. Perhaps the young man who brought him here will know more."

Unwilling to waste even one moment, I took off for the stables hoping this clue would be the one that would lead us to Dan at last. There had to be something on Narcissus—some kind of indicator. Richard followed me into the stables, and we both stared at the prize-winning bay munching hay.

A scrawny young man stepped forward, took off his hat, and took a knee. "Your Highness."

"Rise, sir ..."

"Not sir, just Drumund, Sire."

I forced a grin. "Tell me, Drumund, how did you come across this horse?"

"I was just tending me duties in the field. I found him crying in the thicket. His left side covered in dry blood it was. I nearly fainted, but he sounded so miserable I went and tried to calm the poor beast. I was surprised to see an arrow in his hindquarters. I nearly had me self a shock when I saw it was a black arrow with red feathers. Manic's signature red feathers he got stuck in him."

He held up a broken arrow. Richard took it. It was indeed one of Manic's arrows. Drumund hung his head, "Sire, I didn't see no one with him so I took him home and cleaned him up. I admit I meant to keep him. But when I saw the royal crest on his reins, I knew I couldn't. I nursed him back to health for you though. I hope you will forgive my tardiness of his return."

"Of course, Drumund. Tell me though ... other than the arrow was there anything else on him?"

Drumund fingered his hat. "Just the reigns and saddle, Sire. His bags be empty. I looked."

I put a hand on the young man's shoulder. "It's fine. Thank you for returning him. You have done me a great service. May I return the favor?"

The man's eyes widened. "Do you mean it, Sire?"

"I do. How about since you took such good care of this horse, you continue doing so while you work here at the royal stables?"

Drumund's mouth dropped open and he nodded. With tears in his eyes he bowed. "Thank you, Sire!"

"Find Mr. Kale. He will be your teacher."

The young man bowed and left. I let my smile fade as I turned toward Richard. I took the arrow out of his hand, an uneasiness crawling up my arms like fire ants.

An image of Dan being shot at filled my head, but I pushed it away. Dan was the best knight I knew. He had to be alive. I looked at every inch of Narcissus looking for other clues, but there was nothing other than the arrow. It was just as Drumund had stated.

I clenched my hands and groaned. Nothing was going right. Dan and I were supposed to be celebrating Manic's defeat by now. Manic and his riders were ruining everything and causing all of this pain. Not only for me, but for my people.

"We have to stop him, Richard."

"I know, your Majesty." Richard never called me that unless I was acting more royal than normal, or if he wanted me to.

"Double the patrols, we have to find Manic. Now. I won't have him hurting one more person."

"As you wish, your Majesty," Richard said as he walked out. I rubbed Narcissus' nose.

"Where is your master, boy? Where is Dan?" But I already knew the answer. Dan was either dead, or being tortured by Manic. I clenched my jaw and felt a restlessness rushing through me. Too bad Manic wasn't here right now. If he were, he'd find a dagger in his gullet before he could take a breath to begin gloating.

Edgar and Frederick walked by laughing nearly choking on their giddy moment. I wasn't often jealous of my knights, but at that moment I found I was. Heaving a sigh, I left Narcissus to be cared for by his new stable hand. I attempted to force my boiling blood to slow. But it would not obey. I really did not want to report more bad news to my father. Unfortunately, right now I could see a grand argument in my future.

Unable to take the stress anymore, I darted out of the stables. "Hey, anyone up for some practice?"

"Practice?" asked Edgar raising his eyebrows.

"Yes, the sword," I said, drawing mine and heading for the practice field. I had to do something to calm down this crazy energy before I did something I would undoubtedly regret.

"Are you challenging me, Prince James?" laughed Edgar as he followed after me. "You know I won last time. Easily."

"And a true fight that was," chuckled Frederick.

"Well, it's time I avenged myself," I said through my clenched teeth as I climbed over the fence into the practice field.

Edgar laughed again and pulled out his own sword. "So be it, but you are going to need some new trick up your sleeve to beat me."

I sneered. Yes, I had a new trick. It's called pent-up frustration, and I was ready to unleash it. I'd win this bout of sword fighting, and another, and another until my world settled back down or my sword broke.

Edgar entered the practice field light-hearted, jovial, and confident. I was afraid he wouldn't be feeling the same way in a minute. We both quickly draped on some simple chain mail knowing this was just practice. My other friends Frederick, Roland, and Darwin leaned against the railings to watch.

"I thought you would want witnesses," called Frederick.

"Witnesses to watch him lose to me again," laughed Edgar.

"Or win," I said raising my sword.

"Remember the rules of a practice fight. No death strikes, head strikes, or intentionally drawing blood. Bruises are just a part of the game. Understood?" said Frederick.

Edgar and I nodded.

"Begin!" shouted Frederick.

I attacked more than I defended, and Edgar's eyes widened more than once. He stumbled back a few times, broke into a sweat first, and had to adjust his shield more often than usual.

"Anything you would like to share, James?" he asked as he parried again.

"No."

"Are you sure?" he asked as I pinned him against the railing.

"Quite sure."

He shoved me back hard, and I stumbled backwards into the middle of the practice field.

"Is it the girl?" called Roland from the sidelines.

I shook my head and jumped as Edgar tried to sweep my legs out from under me.

"You are not fooling us, James. We know you have been bent out of shape by her getting hurt and all," said Frederick.

"No, he was going crazy before that," called Darwin with a chortle.

"Is she getting any better, James? Are her memories coming back?" asked Roland.

"No, not yet," I said.

"Is it Dan?" asked Edgar lowering his defenses for a moment. I attacked, and he hardly had time to block my movements.

"It's both," said Richard coming up behind my friends. All eyes turned to me, but I did not want to get into it. I knocked Edgar to the ground and held my sword to his chest.

Edgar smirked, "I yield. I doubt any of us could win today with the mood you're in anyways."

His statement would have offended me if he hadn't been speaking the truth.

I let him up and nodded at Darwin who groaned and climbed into the field.

"Don't worry, James," said Richard. "We will find Dan, and Lady A will get better. You will see."

"Always the optimist," said Darwin, shrugging the chainmail on.

"Well, one of us has to be," Richard said.

I grinned. *Yes, one of us has to be, and it might as well be Richard.*

"Are you ready?" I asked Darwin. He nodded and stood at the ready.

"Fight," yelled Frederick.

Chapter 11

~Lady A~

I knew this castle had a library somewhere, but I couldn't seem to find it. I had been looking for half an hour at least. When I found the entry hall for the third time, I was ready to give up. I turned and started toward my room when a door banged open down the opposite hall. I jumped, convinced that a black-cloaked villain was about to pounce and drag me to my doom.

James and his father emerged instead. I leaned against the wall and waited for my heart to stop attempting to break out of my chest. I didn't mean to eavesdrop, but they weren't talking in low tones so it would have been hard not to hear.

"We have already doubled the patrols father. What else do you want me to do? How were we supposed to know that Tarsh would be a target at the same time as Jude? The scouts were sure the only signs of Manic were in Jude. We were prepared."

"And yet we failed a city—an entire city. You might have been prepared, son, but only for one. Tarsh was nearly burnt to the ground. Manic has upped his torture. A few months ago, he was threatening individual families if they wouldn't join him, and now he is destroying whole villages."

"I know Father, I want nothing more than to stop him. We are doing what we can..."

"We must do more. The Lords are starting to question my ability to rule the land. Which is exactly what Manic wants. I have placated them for the time being, but this cannot continue. I want you to double the guards all day and night! I want scouts in every city, at every cross road, and at every river. I want him stopped. I want him caught."

"Yes, Father," James said adverting his eyes from his father's.

A few breaths later, the King's shoulders slumped. "James, I know you are doing what you can. I hoped he would give up his ridiculous claims, when we have continually stopped his plans. But he has escalated his terror instead. This has gone on for far too long. You will understand more when you are king."

"I know. I will make those adjustments immediately."

They turned the corner at the other end of the hall and I didn't hear any more of their conversation. I felt like cold liquid had been poured into my heart. I was apparently supposed to know how to stop Manic. But I couldn't remember anything. I tried not to cry as I slowly walked in the opposite direction. I searched the dark clouds in my mind, but nothing was there. Why was nothing there? I closed my eyes, fell into a window seat, and groaned. I needed to fix this.

"What are you doing?"

I jumped at Iree's question. "Nothing, Iree."

"No, you're braiding your hair, then ripping it out, then braiding it again. Why are you doing that? It was pretty."

"I don't know why," I admitted looking at the haphazard braid in my hands.

"Maybe that's a clue," she squealed clapping her hands.

"Maybe," I could hear the pent-up tears in my voice. I knew Iree could, too.

"You want to remember, don't you?" she asked, sitting down next to me and putting her gloved hand on mine.

"Of course, I do. But I am also a little afraid because I don't want to remember the scary things that led to me losing my memory. I want to help though, and that makes it worth the pain, right?"

She put her other hand onto the small pile of our hands. "Right. You will remember. I know it. We need to try something different," she said in the calmest voice I had ever heard from her. "Hmm ..." she said tapping her chin. "I know. How about dancing?"

"What?"

"Dancing. You know—one, two, three, one, two, three," she said jumping up and performing a simple step. "You are a Lady of noble birth, surely you learned how to dance. It could be just the thing."

I doubted it. "You never know, Iree," I muttered braiding my hair again.

"Great," she said as she pulled me up and towed me down the hall.

"Iree, where are you taking me?"

"To find your memories! Hopefully."

Iree dragged me into the center of a magnificent ballroom. "Stay here. I will be right back," she declared as she darted off. I shook my head. I loved that silly girl.

I looked around the circular room; the dark brown floors gleamed as if they had been shined only a moment ago. The white arches that held up the second-level balcony, that circled the room, were carved with vines and flowers—the petals were covered in gold. The center of the ceiling in the room formed a great dome. It was painted with a bright blue sky and fluffy clouds. A large chandelier of crystals hung down, catching the light from the second-level windows, making the whole room glimmer.

I didn't stop my feet from moving, on their own, up to the second level. I climbed the winding stair and slowly approached the carved stone railing. I glanced down at the ballroom floor and found I could not look away. It looked almost like stars glittering in the night sky with the dark wood floors acting as the sky, and the reflection from the chandelier providing the sparkling light.

"I could stay here forever," I breathed. I waited, leaning against the railing that crowned the top of one of the lower arches. A few minutes later, a woman entered, walked to a raised dais, and picked up a round-looking instrument with strings. A man followed and he picked up a smaller instrument with strings as well. A few others entered and also picked up instruments. A moment later, Iree bounced in, her curls springing sporadically, pulling her brother, James, behind her.

"Lady A!" she called looking around for me.

"I'm here," I said. My heart started to race the moment I saw James walk into the room. Why did it keep doing that? Iree smiled up at me and waved me down. *I can do this,* I thought. *Maybe this will help.* It wasn't impossible after all. I could have danced every day of my life for all I knew.

I walked down the curved stairs and slowly approached Iree and James. His eyes found mine and I could not turn away. Not that I wanted too.

"Very good, now you take her by the waist," Iree said pushing James forward. "Hold his hand Lady A," she added, her smile dimpling her cheeks.

James looked away from me and dramatically rolled his eyes at his sister. "Yes, dancing mistress."

Iree giggled.

He turned to me and extended his hand. "May I have this dance, My Lady?" he asked.

I felt a warm tingling sensation run down my arms and nodded. He pulled me close as the musicians started to play and placed his hand on my waist. My heart started beating faster and I sucked in a quick breath to try and calm it down, he could probably feel it, or hear it. "James, I'm not sure I know how to ..."

"It's all right," he whispered, a half smile appearing on his face. "Just follow me."

With a hard swallow I nodded and held onto him tight. I didn't know who I could trust at the moment, not really, but I felt like I could trust him, maybe with everything. The thought should have terrified me, but it didn't. I wanted to trust him. If only I could remember if trusting him was actually a good idea.

I was grateful the song was slow. I fumbled a few times, and kept looking at my feet, trying to get them to do what I thought they were supposed to do.

"Lady A," James said with a bit of a laugh in his tone as he let go of my hand and tipped my chin up. I was looking directly at him, only inches from his face. "It will be easier if you don't watch them, trust me."

My breath froze in my chest as I stared into his light blue eyes. He let go of my chin and took my hand again. I could still feel the warmth where his hand had touched. As we danced, I found that my feet did better, but my heartbeat did not. James suddenly smiled and it looked to me like he was trying to hide a laugh.

"What?" I asked.

"Nothing," he said.

"No, tell me, am I terribly ungraceful? Maybe I've never danced before ..." I made to pull away from him but pulled me closer instead.

"No, in fact I am impressed. You have definitely danced before."

"Then what is it?"

"Iree is peeking out from behind an arch. Her smile is as wide as a hunting horn. I think," he said leaning in to whisper in my ear, "that she is trying to play matchmaker."

"Well, she did already ask me if I was going to marry you."

"What?" he said pulling back a bit.

"I told her no, so don't worry. I'm not like the other vampire courtiers who are plotting for your royal blood."

He threw back his head and laughed hard. He twirled me around and when he pulled me close again, he whispered in my ear. "There you are, my Lady A." I felt confused and must have looked it because his smile softened. "You sounded like yourself for a moment there. You never did speak highly of court."

"Oh, am I always so crass?"

He laughed again, "No, I wouldn't say you were ever crass. Just a tease."

"Hmm ... which is why I wouldn't tell you my name?"

"Yes, but I imagine you are only half as bad of a trouble maker as Dan."

I couldn't help it. I smiled at that.

"James, don't we have record of my name? Couldn't we look it up?"

He laughed, but tried to make it seem like a cough. "That particular record is at your home in Veyon. When my parents learned about our little game, they sent the record to you so that I didn't give into temptation and look. And so, no one else would either. I think that they liked our game as much as we did."

"But your parents should know, shouldn't they? They are friends with my parents after all."

"Yes, but my father doesn't pay attention to things he doesn't have to. My mother has tried to remember. She says there are too many nobles to remember all of their names, unless they gave her a reason to remember."

"And I never did."

"You were often away with your parents and never in Saris. And I am afraid you didn't take part in any of their ambassador duties. So, no, that is not until after we started writing. But she didn't try to find out your name because she didn't want to accidentally spoil our fun. She was always the one to change the subject when people brought up the Albons, especially when I was present. And Dan only aided her."

"Oh." I tried not to frown but it was hard to keep it away. I had hoped my simple suggestion would have led to an easy search resulting in finding my name and my memories.

James abruptly spun me around and my lack of attention caught me off guard. I felt my feet tangle up. I lost my grip on his shoulder and was already imagining how it would feel to hit the floor when he caught me, just as the song ended. Our eyes connected. Our faces only an inch or so apart, I struggled to breath normally as he pulled me upright. He cleared his throat, but didn't look away.

"Are you okay?" he asked sounding a little breathless himself.

"Yes, forgive me."

"No, no it was me. I should have warned you."

"Do you think there is any chance Iree will decide that was just an awkward dip?"

He snorted. "Probably."

Iree came bounding over to us and grabbed us both by the middle into a hug. She turned her big, bright eyes up to me. "Anything?"

"I'm afraid not what you were hoping for, Iree, but we did discover that I can dance ... ish." I said looking up at James.

Iree's eyes dropped to the floor.

"Don't worry little sis. She will remember soon enough, especially with you helping her," James said, pulling one of the curls by her face. She glared at him and folded her arms in protest. He smiled back at her. It seemed however that his eyes wanted to stay connected with mine. My cheeks grew warmer with his gaze. I looked away hoping my cheeks would lose their pink shade.

"Maybe if we try a different dance. She might not have ever danced that one," said Iree with new excitement growing in her tone.

I was about to refuse in the politest way I could think of, but Richard stepped into the room saving me the trouble.

"Yes, Richard?"

"Your father wishes to see you, James."

"I don't doubt it." James looked at Iree who had pushed out her bottom lip and was glaring at Richard. "Maybe try something else, Sis. I've got to go."

"I know," she said, her shoulders slumping. If there had been a chair near by, I bet she would have dramatically fallen into it. "But tell father I am very put out, James."

"I will." He turned his eyes back toward me, "Pardon me, My Lady."

I nodded, not sure if my voice would betray the way my heart was pounding.

We both watched him leave, but the moment James disappeared Iree turned her face to me. She was glowing again. "I know what we can do," she squealed. "I have an even better idea! Let's go to the seamstress. I bet all the pretty dresses will help. All girls love dresses." Iree pulled on my good arm and started dragging me out of the room.

I sighed. I guess it couldn't hurt to give it a try. What else was I going to do?

Chapter 12

~James~

"Please, tell me we have some good news to cheer my father up?" I said after Richard and I left the ballroom.

"I'm afraid not, James. Roland says there is no sign of Manic where he and his men have been scouting, and Edgar hasn't returned yet."

"Wasn't he supposed to be back a few hours ago?"

Richard nodded. "I'm sure it's nothing."

"Let's hope so."

I walked into my father's study and could immediately see that something was wrong with him. He was pouring over a map of the kingdom that he had covered in circles and X's. He had what looked like lists strewn all about and his usually tidy clothes were untucked and unbuttoned.

"You wished to see me, Father."

He looked up and eyed Richard. "Leave us."

Richard bowed, turned, and left the room. Usually, my father didn't mind Richard staying for any of our conversations. Something was definitely wrong.

"What is going on, Father?" I said nodding toward the door where Richard had exited.

"I think I have it figured out, son."

"Have you been in here fretting ever since I left you here earlier?"

"Not fretting. Figuring."

"Whatever you say, father."

"Our attempts to capture Manic keep failing us. But how can they all keep failing? Our sources are reliable. Our most trusted men were chosen. Three of your best friends in the world have led the groups at any slight whiff of Manic. We shouldn't have failed, ever. Yet we have failed to apprehend him every single time."

He sat back in his chair and rubbed his forehead. "Son, this has led me to believe that we have an informer, a double-crosser. Someone we trust is on Manic's side."

"What? Who?"

"You agree it makes sense?" he asked, his hair bopping about wildly.

"Yes, I do, but who would do such a thing to us?"

"I don't know," he said, gesturing to the lists of what I saw now were crossed out names. "But I do know that with all of our failed attempts to capture Manic, there has to be a traitor. I won't lie, Son, I immediately thought of Dan. Especially with this whole mess involving his sister."

"What, no, Father it could never be Dan."

"Are you positive? Would you swear to it with your kingdom and all of our people's lives on the line? It was his idea to act as a traitor to his country to get information on Manic. Who's to say he could have easily done that and said he was still on our side."

"It is not Dan. Nor is it Lady A. I would swear on my kingdom, my people, and on my own sword to that."

My father dragged his hands down his face and fell into his chair. He nodded. "Fine. We need to be on the look out, son. We need to be careful with whom we trust information until the informer is found. And he must be found soon or else we will continue to fail. I don't know about you, but I am ready to have all of this become a bad, distant memory."

"As am I, Father."

He picked up one of his papers and looked at me, his mouth as thin as I have ever seen it. "Son, I hate to suggest it—but I think you need to look into your friends."

"Father!"

"Listen. Only Daniel, Edgar, Darwin, Richard, Roland, and Frederick have been privy to all of the same information as we have been. And Richard, Roland, Edgar, and Darwin are the only ones who have had information that no one else had but you and I. You must admit it would be wise to at least check to see if they are all still loyal to us."

"My word isn't enough?"

"I wish it was, but not this time my son. There is a traitor. He is someone who has access to our plans. And he must be found. You agree to that don't you?"

"This is why you asked Richard to leave? You think he could be the one, don't you?"

"I don't know son, but I ..."

"It is not Richard!"

"But it is someone."

I clenched my teeth. I wanted to argue more, but I knew he would want proof to exonerate my friends. And if that was the case then I would look into my friends and prove them all not guilty of treason. "Yes, Father."

He nodded to the door. "Go find him."

I stormed out of the room; angry at the possibility of a traitor and at my father for saying it was one of my friends.

"You look a little tense, Sire?" said Richard. I considered my father's words for half a second before I dismissed them. It wasn't Richard. It could never be Richard. That was one thing I was positive of. I trusted him with my life every day and have since I was three years old. Add the fact that he was hardly ever not by my side. He was eliminated as a suspect right away.

There would have been no time for him to sneak off and join a villain and his traitorous riders. My other friends, however, I hated to admit, could have had the chance. I started walking across the entrance hall, heading toward the barracks.

"Richard, we have a traitor who is making our capture of Manic impossible."

I paused, taking note of his reaction. His eyes hardened a bit but he nodded.

"I'm afraid that makes sense, Sire."

"And Father thinks it is one of our friends."

"James."

"I know. I don't want to think that he is even close to being right, but my head tells me his reasoning is sound. I can't see any of them choosing Manic over us. I trust all of them, but I also know my father is right about the traitor."

Richard put a hand on my shoulder. "What would you like me to do?"

I exhaled a long breath. "Help me look into our friends without them noticing. And if any of them are on Manic's side then we'll ..."

I broke off an unpleasant thought inching its way to the forefront of my mind. Edgar had been gone a long time. And he had returned late a few other times recently.

"What is it, James?"

I sighed, a sense of dread filling my soul. "Keep an extra eye on Edgar."

"Do you think it could be him?" asked Richard his brow furrowing.

"I don't know, but I know he has at least had the opportunity."

"I'll take care of it."

"Thanks, Richard. This I could not do alone."

"You'll never have to, James."

Chapter 13

~Lady A~

Iree and I spent hours in the royal seamstress's rooms. Iree insisted that we breathe in all the fabrics, compare what the different colors did with our complexions, get measured, and design our own dresses. It was entertaining, but nothing came of it.

Nothing I was looking for anyway. No sparks of memory at all. Figuring out that dark blue with gold trimmings would make me a glorious dress didn't help at all. Iree seemed a little disappointed by that news as well, however she gave me a tight hug, thanked me for a wonderful afternoon, and bounced off in her usual manner.

She talked of nothing else at dinner with only the queen and I. James was working with the patrols and the king was busy. Queen Alexia was sweet as always and helped me feel comfortable. I admit I did wish James had been there. It was somewhat strange realizing that I missed him, but I did.

Later that evening, I still felt that desire to see him. In an attempt to push away that ache I walked out onto my balcony. I breathed in the night air and felt some of the tension in my jaw loosen. I found my fingers playing with the ends of my hair of their own accord again. My fingers were halfway through a new braid when I forced my hands to stop.

I wasn't sure why I did that. I was also kind of glad I did. It was something that I knew was all me. Something that was myself for sure, and wasn't clouded by the darkness that hid my current memories.

I pulled my hands away and turned my attention back to the night. My eyes found a group of men approaching the castle. They were all laughing and pushing each other. James tousled a young man's hair who was escorting a horse back to the stables. I took a step back. I wasn't afraid of James or anything, in fact I imagined for a moment that he was on his way to see me. I didn't want him to see me staring though. I turned inside and let their laughter fade away as I closed the balcony door.

"Can I get you anything, My Lady?" asked Netta coming in from the washroom.

"No, thank you, Netta."

"All right, how are you feeling this evening?"

"Just the arm, and my head still aches every now and then, but I think the rest is behind me."

She smiled and patted my shoulder. "Good, well, goodnight My Lady."

"Goodnight."

I watched her leave, but with the snap of the door I felt a small chill shoot through me. I walked to my fire and pulled my robe tighter around myself, but the chill wasn't from the cold. I looked around the darkening corners of my room and felt for the first time alone, scared, and vulnerable. Like I was being watched ny some unknown demon.

Not wanting to be alone with my current thoughts that were quickly turning in an unpleasant direction, I pulled a book off of the side table by my bed. I crawled into my covers with my robe on and moved my candles closer. I read until my eyes kept closing and the paragraph, I was trying to read made no sense after the fifth or sixth time I had read it. I pulled the covers up to my chin and rolled into a ball, letting sleep take me away from the troubles of the day.

Laughter echoed from the darkness. It started quietly sending goose bumps crawling up my arms and legs. I whipped around, but could see nothing through the mist that swirled all around me and held back the light. I batted it away, but the mist only grew thicker.

The laughter continued growing louder and louder until my ears felt like they would burst. I fell to my knees and tried to burry my head in the fabric of my dress to block out the noise.

"Whoever you are leave me alone!" I screamed through the mist. "Leave me alone!" But there was no answer. The laughter only grew.

I gave up on trying to block it out so I stood and turned to run away. But I ran directly into something solid in the darkness and fell. A torch lit and the mist lightened. A man with wild, evil eyes stood before me. They glowed red from the firelight. His orange beard and hair stuck out from his head twisting into a wild mane of burnt-looking tendrils. Lion-like fangs hung from his putrid mouth, which dripped with saliva and wetted his blood-red lips as he threw back his head and continued to laugh.

I clambered to my feet ready to run past the man, but he widened his stance and shook his head. Next to him a hooded black-cloaked figure appeared, its hood concealing his face. Just as I realized he was there another hooded man appeared and another and another. They formed a tight circle around me, opened their mouths, and blew what felt like fiery dragon breath. I fell to my knees.

They stepped closer, encircling me until they were shoulder to shoulder leaving the laughing, wild man and myself in the center. My heart hammered, and I found it hard to breathe.

I scrambled to my feet and tried to push through the wall of cloaked figures, but they only pushed me back as their numbers continued to double making their wall thicker and thicker. I was sure there was no chance of escape.

"Help," I yelped into the darkness. Which only made the cloaked figures join their master in roaring laughter.

"There is no escape," one of them hissed.

"You are done for," added another.

"Manic always gets what he wants!" growled the lion-like laughing man as he began to paw at the ground. I backed away from him until I was touching the wall of black-cloaked men, but they pushed me back into the center of the circle.

"Help me!" I shouted through the laughter. "Help me!" I screamed again. The wild man's red eyes caught mine, and I froze. I couldn't turn away as much as I wanted to. It was as if some kind of dark magic was holding my head making me look at him. Look at my doom.

"I will destroy you!" he bellowed.

"Help me!" I yelled as he charged. "Manic, no!"

*　　　*　　　*　　　*

~James~

After a full day of ordering more patrols, training men, secretly looking for a traitor, and dancing with Lady A, I was exhausted. I lay on my bed fully clothed, chainmail on, sword still in its scabbard, and stared up at my bed hangings. I should have been asleep the moment I fell onto my pillow, but my mind was wide-awake and churning. I thought if I lay there with my eyes closed my mind would quiet as usual, but tonight it did not.

"Forget sleep," I said as I stood up and shrugged out of my chainmail. I began to pace my room hoping to work out my excess energy. It wasn't trouble with Manic that was keeping me up; I had gotten past those sleepless nights. If I hadn't, I would be dead from exhaustion already—it was my conversations about Manic with my father today that kept me awake.

I clenched my teeth thinking about how he had thought Dan could be a traitor. Edgar had seemed normal, but that didn't make him innocent. I still had to consider him. I had observed all of my other friends this evening and I could not see any of them betraying me. If it wasn't one of them, Edgar included, who could it be?

I shook my head and tried to push those thoughts away, but what filled my mind wasn't going to let me go to sleep either—Lady A. If I was honest, half of my frustration bubbling inside of me was because of her.

Seeing her every day was driving me mad. I was already pretty much in love with her from her letters alone, but seeing her face to face every day was intensifying the feeling. And it hurt that she did not know me at all. Not knowing if she could care for me as I cared for her was more than a little vexing.

My mind circled back to the probable traitor and I couldn't take it. My room was far too small for my state of mind. I left; hoping a walk around the halls would calm down my mind.

Richard was still awake and raised his eyebrows as I passed him in the hall. He fell into step behind me as usual. I didn't want a shadow tonight. But it was his job so I tried to ignore him.

After turning a few random corners, he cleared his throat and asked, "Going anywhere in particular, your Highness?"

"No, Richard."

"Are you all right?"

"Yes, I just can't sleep," I said sharply.

"You aren't stressing about the traitor, are you? I promise I am looking into ..."

"No!"

"I yield."

He left it at that—one of the reasons I liked Richard. He knew when to stop asking questions. I didn't pay attention to where my feet were taking me; I was just grinding my frustration into the floor with every step.

I was beginning to feel less crazed when I looked up and saw the guard Egan posted by Lady A's door. I clenched my teeth, and cursed under my breath. I turned to head back down the hall, ignoring Richard's confused face. I was about to stomp away when I heard a scream that shoved what felt like an icicle into my heart.

Richard, Egan, and I all turned toward Lady A's door as a second scream followed the first. Egan yanked her door open and the three of us raced inside. "Check the balcony," I shouted at Richard. Egan ran into the adjoining wash room, and I headed directly to Lady A who was sitting up in her bed, clutching her blanket in a ball under her chin, her eyes shut tight, her head turned away as if she were about to be struck.

"Lady A?" I said rushing to her side. I reached out, softly putting a hand on her shoulder.

She gasped and cringed away as if my hand had been a red-hot poker.

"Lady A, you're okay. It's James." She turned her head slightly, and one gray eye opened to look at me. Then both of her eyes flew open and darted around the room.

"Was someone here? Did they try to hurt you?" I asked as she looked around again, but she shook her head and pulled the covers up to her eyes.

Richard came back in from the balcony. "No sign of an intruder, James." I looked to Egan who had come back into the room as well. He shook his head and shrugged. I looked back at Lady A and heard a sob from behind her blanket.

"Lady A," I said softly, gently placing my hand on one of hers. She was clutching her blanket so tightly her fingers had turned white. "Can you tell me what happened?"

She lowered the blanket just enough for me to see her tear-filled eyes. "I'm sorry," she cried. "I didn't mean to cause a fuss. I'm all right. It was only a dream."

Richard threw his hands in the air, and Egan muttered something that sounded like, "Women." I let out a slow breath and sat on the edge of her bed. I put my arm around her and pulled her to me until her head was leaning against my arm.

"I'm sorry ... I didn't mean to. It was horrible. They were, and I was," she babbled.

"I have a feeling this wasn't any old dream," I said putting aside my own frustration.

"It felt real," she whispered with a shudder.

"Can you tell us about it?" I asked, glancing at Richard, who nodded.

"I didn't mean for you all to run in here. I'm sorry," she said again.

"We know. We aren't angry."

She pulled away from my side and studied me for a moment. My shoulder immediately missed her.

"James ... what does Manic look like?"

"Why do you ask?"

"Please, I need to know. What does he look like?"

I shrugged, "We don't know, Lady A. We haven't been able to meet him face to face yet. And no one seems willing or able to describe him."

"I think I can."

Richard and Egan both took a step forward, their eyes wide as I felt my own jaw fall open. "Are you serious?"

"Yes," she said, a slight sob in her voice.

"Do you remember him? Or Dan's description of him? Is your memory coming back?"

"I don't know for sure, but he was in my dream. I know dreams aren't real, but it had to be him. I know it was him. I saw him clearly. It sounds insane but I know it is true as surely as I know that you are sitting here beside me."

Her eyes pleaded with mine to believe her, and I did. I was sure she'd seen him when she had been chased into the ravine. And I knew Dan would have described him to her. If she said she knew what he looked like then I had to believe her. This is what we had been waiting for.

"Tell me. Describe him."

She swallowed hard. "He is kind of stocky, and has crazy red hair—wild-like, kind of like a lion's mane, with a beard the same color. Dark, bloodthirsty evil eyes. And his men, they wear black cloaks to conceal their identity."

"Yes," I confirmed as she pulled the covers over her face until only her eyes were visible.

"I saw him in my dream laughing at me. They were all laughing. They had me trapped. I was going to die."

I wanted to pull her into a hug again, but wasn't sure if she had pulled away on purpose. It was rather improper for me to be sitting on her bed. So, I stood and walked the few steps over to Egan.

"Send for Netta. She might have an herb or something to help."

Egan bowed and left. Richard took a step closer to me and whispered, "What do you think?"

"I think it's the closest we've ever come to a possible description of him. I think we should trust it."

I glanced back at Lady A. I couldn't see her eyes, but she was still trembling.

"Could she really be remembering? " Richard asked.

"I believe so, but I was hoping she wouldn't start with something like that," I said.

Netta raced into the room a moment later, her hair bows in disarray, and her robe hanging lopsided over her nightdress. Netta threw a case of herbs on the bed and started digging through it. She shooed us away before we could offer any assistance. I looked back from the doorway and saw Lady A's eyes watching me. Almost pleading with me. I gave her the best smile I could muster before I left.

"What happens now?" asked Richard when we were in the hall.

"We must get her description to every scout and every patrol. This will make my father happy, finally," I said.

"And Lady A?"

"I say we try to help her remember more. It's strange that a horrible thing has made more progress than all the good things Iree keeps trying," I said with a frown.

"I know, and the princess has been trying really hard."

I turned to him, "Maybe that one bad dream was stronger than the rest of the things we've tried. Maybe what she needs is something scary, not nice."

"It is unfortunate that we don't know a harmless, bad experience to throw her into to see if everything would come back," Richard said. "Not that we would wish unfortunate experiences on the Lady."

I stopped walking and drugged my hands through my hair. "Richard, I do know of a harmless, terrible experience we could try. If Lady A knew what I was thinking though, I am afraid she would have me run through. But if we need to scare her memories back then I know the perfect thing." I started walking faster this time. "Come on, we have to talk to my parents right away."

"What are you going to do?"

"Give my father a reason to smile and convince my mother to help me get Lady A's memory back."

"How?"

"Tomorrow Lady A is going to court—the one place I know she fears."

Chapter 14

~Lady A~

Iree looked like she was about to burst as she leaned on the dresser watching Netta pull my hair up into some kind of intricate web of braids and curls. I doubted the talented maid would be able to hide the wound on my head that was still healing, but somehow, she managed it with some carefully placed flowers.

I looked at myself in the mirror and gulped. A part of me wished she hadn't done so well and I would have an excuse to stay in my room. I knew I didn't have to be afraid, but I found a trembling coursing though my bones. I kept trying to convince myself that it was leftover fear from my haunting dreams last night, but I knew better. The trembling went deeper than I could comprehend in my current state of mind.

Queen Alexia walked in with a dress folded over her arm. I forced a smile to my lips hoping no one but myself saw how I truly felt.

"I think this one will fit you. It's one of my old lucky court dresses and back in fashion, I believe," the Queen said holding up a beautiful purple dress with gold trimming.

"I love it," giggled Iree touching the sleeve. "You'll look so pretty in it! Can I wear it sometime, too, Mamma?"

"Perhaps Iree, unless Lady A wants to keep it."

"Oh no, how could I? It's a family dress," I said smiling at Iree who brightened.

"You could be family one day you know," she said taking the dress from her mother, holding it against herself, and swaying in front of the mirror.

"She does have a point," said the queen with a soft squeeze on my shoulder. I blushed. "I wish I could have come with you, my lovely girls. But I'm afraid that the boring affairs of the kingdom come first for the queen."

"Don't worry, I'll look after Lady A," said Iree tossing the dress on the bed.

"I know," said the queen accepting Iree's quick hug. "Have a lovely time, ladies," she said as she left.

"I got to go to court for the first time three months ago when I turned twelve," gushed Iree as soon as the door closed. "You are going to love it! They have snacks and tea, and everyone talks about important things and," her face went a little pink, "the girls try to come up with ways to get close to my brother. They think that one of them can get him to propose on the spot." She giggled; her cheeks still a little pink.

"Oh, do they?" I asked as the tightness in my stomach loosened a bit. Iree had that affect on people.

"Yes, they keep trying even though he hasn't come close to proposing even once. My brother is smart enough to know what they are up to, so don't worry. It's so great."

"It sounds fun, Iree," I said, but for some reason I doubted it. I had this feeling of knots being tied in my stomach, and my dry throat made it hard to swallow. I wanted to refuse going and curl up on my window seat, but I knew I had to go. James had been so excited about the idea. Add Iree's giddy mood and how could I refuse? I had no reason to fear this. It wasn't like Manic would be hiding under a table or anything. *Shake it off, Lady A*, I told myself. *This might be the thing to make your memory come back.*

Netta and Iree helped me into the queen's borrowed dress and a few minutes later I was declared perfect. I looked at the small wrap still around my left hand, but I knew there was nothing that could be done about that.

"Come on," Iree said, pulling on my good arm. "I'm so glad Mamma said I could walk with you. James said he was worried you wouldn't like court, but you will. Trust me."

She pulled me out of my room and continued jabbering about court as if it were a fairy land, but I felt my throat constrict tighter with every step we took. *Come on*, I told myself. *It can't be worth all of this tension. It's just the royal courtiers.*

"Wait until they see you," Iree suddenly declared, her big, bright eyes looking me up and down. "Rosetta will have a fit. She keeps telling the girls they are welcome to try and win the prince but, in the end, he will choose her. She says it's good for them to try to capture his heart so that he is surer of his love for her, or something like that."

"Is she someone he likes?" I asked, a different feeling joining the churning of my stomach.

She paused mid bounce, "Hmm … I don't know."

I felt my shaky smile falter and Iree put a hand on my shoulder, "He likes you more for sure, so don't worry."

She giggled again and pulled me through the entrance hall, down another, and directly into a large room that was full of fifty or sixty people. I pulled back and she paused with me, her bright, blue eyes darting around the room.

Soft chairs and tables holding punch and cakes were dotted about the room. Carved pillars, like the ones in the ballroom, held up the painted ceiling. The room was brightly lit because of the walls that opened up on two sides so all could take in the splendor of the maze gardens.

The lords and ladies were all standing about talking in various clumps. Iree let go of my hand and raced to a small group of girls her size that squealed when she arrived. I felt my throat constrict again. My heart rate went up to the point where I could feel my pulse pounding in my veins. *Why was I acting this way? I had no need to fear this, did I?* I took a deep breath but still the frazzled feeling remained. I was about to back up out of the room and take a few moments to gather my courage or run away all together, when I felt someone slip his hand into mine.

I turned and found myself looking at James. He interlaced his fingers with mine and gave my hand a squeeze. My throat loosened and I could breath again. "May I escort you?" he asked.

"Yes, please," I said, unhappy at the slight trembling in my voice.

He looked into my eyes and squeezed my hand, "You don't have to be afraid, Lady A."

"I'm not," I said even though I knew I was for some foolish reason. He narrowed his eyes at me. "Okay maybe a little," I admitted. "I don't even know where this trepidation is coming from."

He opened his mouth to respond, but then pressed his lips together. He seemed to swallow what he was going to say and said instead, "You can do this." From the way he said it, I wasn't sure if he was talking to himself or me.

We walked further into the room and a group of women immediately turned and flocked toward us. A dark-haired beauty in a bright red dress was smiling the sunniest, even as she eyed me from my flower-filled hair to my toes. Her smile tightened when she spotted our clasped hands.

"Who is this?" asked a pinch-lipped, blond lady in a gold dress.

"This, Mariel, is the Lady Albon, Sir Daniel's sister. Lady A, I would like you to meet four of the loveliest ladies of the court. Mariel, Rosetta, Isabelle, and Cora."

I inclined my head to them, not trusting my voice or a curtsey. They returned the gesture. *Loveliest ladies? Did James fancy them?* I looked at Rosetta. She did have the look of a queen. I felt a pang in my heart at the same time my stomach constricted. I tightened my grip on James's hand. Rosetta's eyes turned cold. Her smile twisted from cynical to tightly polite.

"My goodness, Lady Albon, why haven't we met before?" asked Mariel, her eyes smoldering as she glared at our clasped hands.

"This isn't an interrogation Mariel," said Rosetta shooting Mariel a hard look. If Mariel's eyes were smoldering then Rosetta's were on fire. She strode to my other side and linked her thin, nearly translucent white arm around my bandaged one. "We are pleased you could finally join us, Lady Albon," she said through clenched teeth.

"I am sure you have so many stories to tell from your life with the ambassadors. What an adventurous time you must have had with such amazing parents like yours," said Cora with a dreamy look on her face. I found myself wishing it was Cora who had my arm instead of Rosetta.

"Yes, thank you," I mumbled, unsure of what else to say.

"Come, let me introduce you to the other girls. James, if I may?" said Rosetta flashing him quick smile, her eye lashes fluttering like a hummingbirds wing.

He squeezed my hand and let go; my hand immediately felt cold. "Thank you, Rosetta, I think that is a wonderful idea," he said. I looked at him trying not to appear as terrified as I suddenly felt. He winked at me and walked a short way off and started chatting with what looked like a few friends. His back turned to me.

I felt abandoned. All the nervousness that he had chased away with his arrival returned, but it felt stronger than before as if it had gained strength while it was away. I felt myself start to tremble as I was pulled a few feet away. Why did he leave me? How could he? I needed him to get me through this.

"Ladies, I would like you to meet Lady Albon. Sir Daniel's sister," Rosetta said as she pulled me closer to a larger group of women. Mariel, Isabelle, and Cora followed us. The girls inclined their heads and a few muttered a half-hearted welcome.

"Thank you," I said, forcing my lips into a smile. I noticed Rosetta was taking on the role as my new escort, though I wasn't quite sure why.

The girls started talking one on top of the other in what sounded like nonsense to me. Though many of them found the conversation funny, I couldn't follow it. I looked away from the group and found Iree tasting the punch and giggling with her friends. Was it shameful that I would rather be with her, than this group? Iree saw me staring and smiled but she returned to her friends.

"My dear Lady A, what an interesting choice of … arm jewelry," said Mariel, pointing to my wrapped hand.

"Oh, good heaven's Mariel, no one would wear a filthy rag to court as an accessory. That is unless Lady A is trying to gain some sympathy from the prince. That's it isn't it? Is it?" she said slapping my arm. I barely hid my gasp. "You are a little naive dear, if you thought that would work."

"I thought she was trying to match her hardly in style dress."

"Oh Mariel, you are far too funny for your own good," laughed Rosetta.

I opened my mouth to try and explain, but the girls were already sniggering at the state of another girl's dress. I took the opportunity to leave Rosetta's group a few minutes later when some of the girls broke off and went to the food tables. I had just sampled the punch when Iree came bounding up to me.

"So?"

"Court is … interesting."

"Of course, it is! I think so, too," she said grabbing a cookie and skipping back to her friends.

I looked for the prince as I took another sip of punch. I found him by the doors with Edgar, Frederick, and Darwin. They were chuckling about some story that Frederick was telling. I smiled as I watched the prince with his friends. But my smile faded as Rosetta brushed past me, deliberately making sure her skirts hit mine. She gave me a glare that felt like she had actually pulled my hair as she walked by.

She sauntered over to the prince, linked her arm through his, and looked at me as if staking her claim. Now I understood why she had acted the way she did. She joined in on the laughter, but she kept her eyes on me. It was impossible to miss her point.

I turned away and surveyed the rest of the room. Clusters of people stood about eating and talking; one small group near the fireplace was embroidering. I felt a small urge to move their way but they didn't look any friendlier than Rosetta.

I started slowly walking back toward the door. I had tried court and I didn't think it was going to give me any memories. I didn't like it; I was ready to leave. I turned in an attempt to head out the door when Richard walked up to me.

"Hello, Lady A."

"Hello, Richard, excuse me I ..."

"I think, Lady A, that the prince could use your help," he whispered.

"What do you mean?" I said, my eyes on the floor. I forced away the feelings of what my heart felt like seeing Rosetta on his arm.

He nodded back into the room. Reluctantly, I turned to see Rosetta pulling James out into the maze garden. "She has been telling people all week that she is going to make the prince propose to her today—no matter what she had to do."

"And he won't like that?" I said suddenly feeling like I wanted to slap James and hug him at the same time.

"Really, Lady A? You know him better than that."

Did I? I wasn't so sure. I turned my flaming eyes toward the gardens watching as they disappeared into the hedges.

"But what could I possibly do?" The prince was obviously welcoming her attention. A true friend wouldn't impose on another in the garden, would they?

"Rescue him of course," he said, holding out his arm. I hesitantly took it and let him lead me across the room and outside in the direction that Rosetta had pulled James. "He doesn't like her, Lady A, he never has. He is only nice to her because honestly that is just how James acts. "

Feeling somewhat relieved, I fell into step with him. Richard wasn't one to lie.

"Are you sure we should be doing this?" I asked as we entered the hedges.

"As his bodyguard, it is my duty to follow him everywhere, and no one said I couldn't bring a friend."

"Right," I relented. But only because I wanted to make sure Rosetta wasn't a real vampire courtier. Regardless, I was sure she was willing to trick James into something he didn't want.

We tiptoed through the hedges following Rosetta's tinkling laugh.

"Where are you two going?"

I jumped and Richard placed his hand on his sword. Edgar stood there smiling at us.

"Just following James as usual," Richard said, eyeing Edgar. "What about you?"

"Me? I was curious why everyone seems to be sneaking into the gardens today."

Richard scrutinized Edgar a little more than I thought was necessary but finally nodded. We continued walking with Edgar following closely behind us. When we heard Rosetta's voice all three of us ducked down behind some bushes and peered through the leaves.

Rosetta was walking closer to the prince who was backing himself up into a corner. Her red dress swished softly, and it looked like she was sticking her lips out, so they were more obvious while she talked. She was pretty, but the look in her eyes wasn't. It was like a fox who had cornered the prize chicken.

"James, let us stop pretending. I love you, and I know you love me. I know you want to catch Manic and all, but being engaged won't stop you. And think about how I could plan the whole wedding for the Spring while you are busy. You're sure to catch him by then. And you wouldn't have to do a thing. Not one, except ask me a special question of course."

"You'd better get over there, Lady A," said Richard, giving me a little shove.

"And do what? He's a prince, a knight, and I'm ..."

Richard gave me a pointed look. "You are his Lady A!"

I huffed. That was no answer.

"I'll stay with Lady A. Richard if you want to ..." Edgar started but stopped as Richard turned scorching eyes toward him.

"No, she needs to be the one."

"Why me? You are his bodyguard," I said, watching Rosetta take a step closer to James.

"I know and I am trying to protect him. I doubt she will back off for us. She doesn't know you, and hasn't figured you out yet. You will throw her off her guard. Edgar keep watch." Richard grabbed my arm and led me away from the bushes.

"And stay away from Edgar for now, all right," he whispered.

I was about to ask why when he pushed me around the hedge and I ended up stumbling a few feet down the path right into the gap between the hedges. Rosetta and James both stood there staring right at me.

My face, no doubt, matched Rosetta's dress perfectly in that moment. "I am so sorry. I got ... lost. I hope you can forgive me; I didn't mean to interrupt anything."

"You didn't," said James darting around Rosetta. Rosetta clenched her teeth and I swear she silently snarled at me, her face definitely becoming a closer shade to her dress.

"Are you all right?" James asked coming toward me.

"Yes, I am fine," I said a little harsher than I meant. I suppose I was still a little hurt he left me earlier. I took a deep breath and adopted a pleasanter tone. "I was exploring the maze, but I can't seem to find the way out."

"You are here by yourself unescorted?" seethed Rosetta.

I shrugged.

"Rosetta and I would love to walk you back. Isn't that right, Rosetta?"

"Of course," she said through clenched teeth snaking her arm through his and glaring at me. James offered me his other arm and we all walked out of the gardens together, none of us saying anything. I expected to see Edgar and Richard in the bushes, but they were not there.

"It's easy to find your way out. The path that has the yellow stones every few feet lead from the entrance to the center of the maze," he said pointing out the stones.

"I'll remember that," I said as we followed the path.

"Here we are," said James as we emerged from the hedges a few minutes later. "The secret is simple …" he was going to say more but stopped short. A little way from where we stood Richard was holding up Edgar by his collar. I couldn't tell what they were saying, but the look on their faces was enough to tell us this was more than a casual fight.

"Excuse me, ladies," said James as he took off after his friends. We watched as James confronted his friends and convinced Richard to set Edgar down.

"So brave, isn't he?" sighed Rosetta. "He will make a fantastic king don't you think? He is so loyal and handsome."

"Yes, he is," I said, not looking away from the scene.

"Lady Albon, I want to ask you something," said Rosetta as she pulled on my arm. She led me to a bench carved with winding flowers that sat in front of the fountain that looked like a pot of overflowing wild flowers spilling into a pool of water.

"I've heard that you are the royal family's special guest?" she said as she sat and patted the spot next to her. Not knowing what else I could do, I joined her.

"Yes, I am for now."

"I imagine that you and James are good friends?" she asked, her translucent hand patting mine.

"Yes. Kind of?" Her eyes rose. "I'm sorry, it is hard to explain. I doubt the prince explained my situation. I ran into some trouble recently and was hurt. I have a head injury, and I can't seem to remember things very well."

Rosetta's smile tightened making her eyes squint a bit. "Oh dear, that is so sad. Let me guess, that is the true reason for the wrap?" she said gesturing to my arm. I nodded. "You poor dear. You must let me know if I can be of help."

"Thank you, Rosetta, that is sweet of you to say," I said. A slight smile inching up my face. Maybe Rosetta wasn't all that bad.

"Of course, my dear! What kind of queen will I be if I don't take an interest in others," she laughed, her smile growing even tighter.

"Right," I said. I take it back; I didn't like her at all.

"Oh, you are too cute. I believe you are two years younger than James and I, right?"

I smiled, "I don't know."

"You are Sir Daniel's younger sister, are you not?"

"Yes," I said, feeling a growing unease.

"Great, then allow me introduce you to your newest best friends, just your age and in need of another group member. You'll fit right in."

She yanked me up as she stood. "Come on." I looked toward James, Richard and Edgar who were talking calmer now but didn't look nearly finished. I sighed and followed Rosetta inside and over to the group of girls who were all embroidering as they chatted.

"I have a new friend for your group, ladies. This is Lady Albon, and she loves embroidery."

The girls smiled at me and handed me cloth and a wad of strings.

Rosetta pushed me down into a chair and leaned in to whisper in my ear. "This is your place now. It would be best for you to remember that. And stay away from James. He is mine." I felt my face fall as Rosetta sauntered away and stood next to Mariel, Isabelle, and Cora. They began whispering and made no effort to keep their eyes averted from me. They were a tight group almost as much as the wad of threads I held in my hand.

I sat with my embroidery supplies in my hands and watched the other girls as they silently stitched. Half of me wanted to throw the embroidery in Rosetta's face and storm out of the room, but the other half of me was curious if I would like this. It didn't look that hard.

I guess this will be less scary than anything else I could be doing the rest of this afternoon, I thought.

And that included standing up to Rosetta.

I threaded my needle and positioned it underneath the fabric. I paused for a moment because this felt strangely normal. I began stitching and was surprised how straight my stitches were turning out. I must have done this before. I showed the lady next to me. She offered me a bright smile then went back to her own work, her nose only inches away from her stitches. Feeling happier than I had all day, I continued stitching.

"James," a voice shouted a quarter of an hour later. As James, Richard, and Edgar reentered the room, mine weren't the only eyes following their movements. It seemed every female in the room was focused on them.

"Hey, Roland!" said James his smile improving. Roland bounded over to James and the men slapped each other on the back. "Roland you're back from patrols early."

"I couldn't miss a day at court or else all the ladies would go after you instead of me." The group of friends laughed and launched into talking about plans for a practice session.

I turned back to my embroidery and had just decided it needed another daisy when an arm slid along the back of my chair.

"Hello, Lady A," I looked up to see Roland's face only inches from my own. I couldn't stop the gasp that escaped me.

He smiled and looked at me strangely as if I were something he wanted to eat.

"Hello?" I managed. "Have we met?"

"Yes. I'm Roland, remember? I was one of the knights who helped rescue you from that dreadful inn."

"I remember," I said quickly, not liking that he called the inn dreadful. Wendy and Charles had been nice. In all honesty, they had been the ones to actually do the rescuing. "You are one of James's friends."

He nodded but then looked around and lowered his voice, "Still not remembering much at all I hear."

"I'm afraid not," I said, my stomach tightening a bit.

"Not a thing, huh, I bet that is awful," he said. "Especially when you had something important to say. So, James claims. How tragic that you can't remember it."

"Yes, Roland, and I am sure she doesn't need to keep being reminded about that," said James from right behind us.

"Of course," Roland said as he stood and moved away. "I was just checking up on her." Roland walked away and turned his charms on a group of courtiers at the food table a few feet away."

"Sorry about that," James said eyeing Roland.

"No need to worry," I said, threading my needle with green but not looking up at him. I didn't want him to see my furrowed forehead.

He was about to say more I was sure, but Rosetta showed up. "Come with me James, please? We didn't get to finish our walk earlier."

"I would, but Lady A..."

Rosetta huffed her eyes resembling flaming torches. "Will be fine without you. She isn't some ill-bred ruffian or a new twelve-year-old courtier. She doesn't need you to escort her all day."

I gasped as a sharp pain shot through my head as a memory filled it. A bad memory. Something I was positive I would have been glad to forget forever.

"Lady A?" asked James reaching out for me.

I knocked his hand aside, dropped my embroidery, gathered my skirts, and raced out into the hallway. Hardly looking at where I was going, I fled. All I knew was that I needed to get out of there. Now.

Chapter 15

~Lady A~

I turned right into a hall a few feet away from the courtier's room, caught my foot on my long skirt, and fell. Unwilling to get up and run again, I crawled to the wall and pulled my legs up under my chin and let the tears fall. This was as good a place as any to cry.

There were images in my head. Actual images. Not the muddy blackness I had gotten so used to. This wasn't like the other times where I had known a fact to be true, like that I had embroidered or danced before. I was actually seeing a memory. Why did it have to be a horrible one? One that hurt me to the point where my chest burned, and I could only breathe in heaves.

"Lady A?" shouted James. I heard his footsteps running toward me, but I couldn't unbury my face from my knees.

"Lady A, what happened?" he asked crouching down by me. I moved my head an inch so that I could look at him through my tearful eyes.

"Did someone say something to hurt you? Did Rosetta? Roland? Someone else?" he asked, his face lined with concern.

"A long time ago, someone else did," I said watching his face closely. His eyes grew hard, and his jaw tightened for a bit. Then he must have realized what I actually said and his eyes grew wide.

"You remembered something?"

I nodded reburying my face.

"An actual something ... or more than a little something?"

"One horrible memory, but clearer than the crystal everyone was drinking punch from."

He let out a long breath and sat by me, his back against the same wall. He carefully extracted one of my hands and held it tight in his own.

"I'm sorry. Any chance you want to tell me about it?"

I shook my head. "Don't you need to get back to Rosetta?"

He coughed, "No, please. I'd rather not. Talk to me, Lady A. It will help. I promise."

"It's a bad memory. I don't want to remember it, or talk about it, or anything," I said reburying my face in my dress.

"Lady A, talking about it will help lessen the hurt, I guarantee it. Maybe it will even help you remember more. Hopefully, something good this time."

I knew he was probably right, he usually was, but it still hurt to think about it. I took a deep breath and let it out slowly.

"I was twelve."

"Twelve?" he said surprised. "A much older memory."

I felt my mouth twitch and I raised my head a bit. I looked down the hall. No one was in sight, and so I turned to him taking his other hand as well.

"You promise not to laugh or ..."

"I will merely listen, I promise," he said, squeezing my hands.

"Okay. I was twelve and it was time for my first day at court. I remember they set up a Spring, Summer or Fall welcome event that year for the new courtiers. Mother was supposed to be home in time to escort me to mine."

"Which season was it? Sorry, I said I'd only listen."

"You're fine … um ... I think it was Spring."

He smiled and indicated for me to continue.

I looked at my fingers entwined with his and drew strength from them. "But mother didn't make it in time. I was so nervous I nearly didn't go, but my governess wouldn't hear of it and asked Dan to be my escort instead. He agreed but only because he was expected to. He was only fourteen and really didn't want to deal with taking care of his little sister."

I paused; how did I know that? It must have been buried back somewhere in the slush of my mind. I smiled and James squeezed my hand.

"Anyway, I went all dressed up, and slightly excited, but the moment Dan and I walked through the door he took off to find his friends and left me standing at the doorway. I was alone and unsure of what to do. I slipped into the room, but all I could see were the other girls with their mothers and the young boys with their fathers. I had no one by my side."

I gulped at this next part of the memory, and James squeezed my hand again. "There was a strict, mean-looking lady who was walking about correcting postures and talking to the parents. Do you remember her?"

"I'm guessing it was our Mistress of Manners, Ms. Mellark. She lives and breathes for the new courtier parties."

"She found me. I was staying quiet in the corner not bothering anyone and trying to figure out what I should do. Her eyes caught mine from across the room, and I remember her lips thinning out into a straight line, as her eyes grew dark. I remember trembling as she stormed my way, but I was unable to move."

"Where is your escort?" she had demanded. I didn't know what to say so I didn't say anything. "Straighten up, shoulders back, we do not slouch in the corner like some ill-bred ruffian. Where is your escort?"

James's jaw dropped. "Rosetta didn't mean to ... she couldn't have known …"

"You said you wouldn't interrupt."

"Right, I'm sorry, go on."

"I remember opening my mouth to try and explain, but nothing came out. She grabbed my arm and pulled me into the center of the room. "Whose ill-mannered child is this?" she had demanded in a loud voice. When everyone turned to look, I started to cry. I remember I looked for Dan, but he was nowhere in sight. He was probably off causing trouble with you in the maze or something.

"Straighten up, young lady, turn off the tears; this is not how we behave at court," she had said. "See here, all of you. This is the best example of what I could show you, how not to act. Now, point out your escort young lady or I will have to send you out."

"I looked at the other new twelve-year old's and the group of older courtiers who had stopped to watch. I saw most of them giggling behind their fans or behind their friends' shoulders."

"I don't have one," I had stumbled out."

"Speak up, has no one taught you any manners at all?" I remember I tried to pull away, but she held on tight. 'No one claims her then? Fine, we have no proof you are supposed to be here at all. You certainly don't act like a lady,' she had said as she marched me to the door and threw me out into the hall. A roar of laughter followed me."

I looked down the hall and James followed my gaze. "I sobbed into that rug there for who knows how long."

"And then?" he asked gently, turning my chin away from the rug.

"That's where the memory ends. That's the day I stopped going anywhere I didn't have to. The day I vowed to never return to court. Or visit the castle, ever. And now that is exactly where I am."

He pulled me into his arms and held me. I could hear his heart thumping in his chest and his arms around me made the memory hurt less. In fact, it felt wonderful being in his arms. "I hope Dan got a strong talking to when your mother returned."

I laughed a bit. "Me too."

"That is the longest memory you've had. I'm sorry it had to be an unpleasant one. I'm sorry going to court caused this hurt."

"I didn't think this idea would work. Just like anything else we've tried. Did you know I had been to court before?"

He cleared his throat and said, "I knew you had been once, and I also knew that your one experience was the reason you had never been back. But I didn't know what had happened."

I pulled back and looked at him in the eyes. "That was cruel of you to insist I go. You know that?"

"I do, but I hope you will forgive me. I was only trying to trigger your memory, and it worked … a little." I glared at him and moved until my back was flat against the wall, but he was right.

"Do you think it's really coming back?" I asked a moment later. I thought of the frustrated look the king always gave me when he saw me. He tried to hide it, but knowing I held the key to bringing down Manic, and was unable to tell them what I knew deep inside, was taking quite a toll. Our people were dying every day.

"It's starting to look that way," he said, moving a stray curl off of my cheek. My cheeks grew warm at his touch, and I blurted the first thing that came to my mind.

"I'm surprised that no one followed us out here."

"I told Richard to keep them back." He said his fingers lightly brushing my face.

"And Rosetta obeyed?"

"I know, shocking. But Richard has never let me down."

"Did you know Rosetta fancies herself your queen?" I said, trying to keep the subject away from my lack of memory. But the moment I said it I wished I could take it back. What an awkward thing to say. I knew it was because I didn't want to think about my own failings anymore, but honestly, I could have said something better.

He laughed. "Yes, I did, how could I not?"

"And?" I couldn't help myself asking.

"And she can think anything she wants, but she won't be my wife, my queen, my anything. She doesn't have my heart."

"Someone else does?" I whispered looking up at him.

His expression softened as he looked back at me. "Yes, someone else does."

His gaze held my eyes for a moment and I felt the hurt and the worry melt away.

"Thanks, by the way," he said taking my hand again.

"For what?"

"Saving me from Rosetta earlier."

"Anytime," I said smiling at our clasped hands.

Chapter 16

~Lady A~

It had been eleven days since I had awoken with no memories—eleven dark, confusing, and yet wonderful days. I was enjoying my time at the castle, but I knew it wasn't always going to be like this. I wanted it to be but without my cloudy mind.

I watched the wind blowing the tree branches outside of my window and wished I could feel the wind on my cheeks. I leapt up and was out the door before I realized my feet were moving by themselves. Egan, my bodyguard, fell into step behind me as I raced to the nearest door that led outside.

The wind hit my face the moment I burst outside, and I breathed deeply. An image of swaying leaves filled my mind, and I smiled at the possible memory. I kept my eyes closed and focused on the thin leaves in my mind and swayed with them.

"Dancing alone in the wind?" laughed James.

I jumped as he appeared seemingly out of nowhere. Egan was chatting quietly with Richard near the castle doors. I guess in my haste I didn't even see them nearby.

"No, not really. I was dancing with the leaves."

"Leaves?"

"I had this image of leaves dancing in the wind, and I was trying to hold onto it to see if more memories would follow. But someone interrupted me."

He laughed. "Oh, dear. I shall now forever be blamed for the delay of your memories."

"That's right. How dare you do such a thing. Everyone knows that leaves are the key to memory issues," I said, trying to fight my grin.

"Quick," he said, grabbing my hands and spreading them out wide. "Pull the image back and dance with the leaves again." He spun us both around, and I laughed. I loved the way the wind felt as we twirled together.

He stopped and steadied us both—placing his forehead against mine as we caught our breath.

"Did we salvage it?" he asked, pulling back just far enough for me to look into his eyes.

I frowned, "Forget it, it's too late. The memory is gone."

But a better one is in its place, I thought.

He moaned, but couldn't keep a distraught face for long. "May I at least attempt to make amends by asking you to accompany me on a walk?"

"You may attempt, but we will have to see if you succeed."

The wind blew a stray hair into my face, and James swept it back behind my ear. He left his hand there for a moment, and I felt my skin tingle underneath his warm touch. I wanted to close my eyes and freeze time for a moment, but such thoughts were impossible. I wondered if he wanted to kiss me. He might have, but I wasn't sure. Feeling unexpectedly nervous, I took a step back instead. James dropped his hand to his side.

If my movement bothered him, he didn't show it. He performed an exaggerated bow and offered me his arm. I took it. How could I not? I felt a smile tugging at the corner of my lips and was glad that my nervousness could fade away so quickly.

"Where would the lady like to walk today?" he asked, his smile was warm and comforting, and I relaxed a bit more.

"I'm not sure. This is your castle; any suggestions?"

"Let's see, you've already seen the gardens and most of the castle interior. I know, how about we walk along the top of the surrounding castle wall?"

I looked toward the entrance gates and the thick wall that surrounded the castle and gardens. Torches were being lit as the waning sun dipped closer to the distant hills.

"Sounds perfect."

We walked arm in arm to the castle wall, and the guards at the gate bowed as we passed. James led me up a winding staircase in one of the towers and up onto the wall. I gripped James's arm a little tighter as I spotted the city now below us. Guards were stationed up here as well.

"Do they ever get bored?" I asked out loud and then gasped because I hadn't meant to.

James chuckled, "Absolutely. I've taken my fair share of guard duty shifts to know that."

"The prince is also a guard?"

"A knight must do what is needed to protect the kingdom," he said.

I studied him for a moment and shook my head, "No, you lost a bet, didn't you?"

"I did not. What makes you say such a thing?" He turned away from me, and I let go of his hand and stepped in front of him.

"Come on, James, you are the prince. I'm not buying that."

His smile widened. "Fine, yes I did."

"Was it to Dan?"

He groaned and started walking again. "You didn't remember that did you?"

"No, but now I wouldn't mind hearing about it," I said as I caught up to him.

"That's okay, I'll pass."

"It can't be that bad," I laughed, raising my eyebrow as far as it would go. Maybe he'd get the hint.

He looked around us to make sure no one was in earshot. Egan and Richard were following us but were a few paces behind. "All right, but you must swear not to say anything. Ever."

"Now I am really intrigued."

"We were being silly boys. It was nothing."

"It doesn't sound like nothing. And you never know, something in your story might trigger my memory."

He looked at me like I had lost my mind, which in fact I did. "I suppose the story could make up for you disrupting my dancing with leaves." I said waggling my eyebrows at him.

He shook his head. "I can't believe I am going to tell you this."

"Go on."

"Ahh … Dan and I were a few months away from being knighted, and everything between us was a competition. Since I was the prince, I felt I was required to be the best. The strongest, fastest, quickest at everything and I was, or so I thought. But one-night Dan got all huffy about something that I can't remember now and burst out that I was only the best at everything because he had been holding back."

"Oh no. To make you look good?"

"Exactly. I was furious when he said that. I called him a liar, amongst other things that I would not repeat in front of a lady. So, he challenged me to prove it with a test."

"Really? He'd challenge the prince?"

Who was this brother of mine anyway? I was really starting to wish I knew.

"It's not strange coming from Dan. Anyway, he said the loser had to do a week's worth of guard duty and the winner would always know he was the best, even if it was only between the two of us."

"What did you have to do?" I laughed. "Wrestle a giant? Chase a cheetah?"

He sighed, "If only. No, we were dumb boys and came up with a much crazier idea."

"James, wasn't this only a little over a year ago?"

"A little more than that."

He stopped walking and we leaned against the wall looking over the city below us. He reached for my hand and interlaced our fingers. "The sun will be setting at any moment."

"No, sir. No changing the subject. I want to know how you lost this bet."

He hung his head. "You already know I lost so what does it matter? Dan was obviously better."

"Not by much I am sure. What happened?"

He kept my hand in his as he turned to face me, and I was glad he came a little closer. "We came up with an outrageous test.

We had to do a sequence of events to test our skills. We started off with swimming across the moat, next climbing up the wall, running down it about a quarter mile, climbing down the other side of the wall into the stable area. After that we had to fully saddle a horse, take a bow and only two arrows. We rode to where we had targets set up, and then we had to hit the bulls-eye with only two shots. The first one done was the winner."

"Wow."

"I know. Dan won, but I challenged the outcome by saying it wasn't fair because Narcissus was a faster horse than Dante. I argued that the results would have been different if I'd had Narcissus. Dan did have the better horse that we all agreed to. He claimed I would have lost anyway because it took me two shots to hit the bulls-eye, and he got it in one."

"How in the world did you both do all of that with no one noticing?

"We did it in the middle of the night. But Richard, Roland, Edgar, Frederick, and Darwin were all there as witnesses. I was so embarrassed to have been beaten. Dan, however, really was the best."

"And your friends didn't tease you about it?"

"Not much. They are great like that. But every time we were approached and told that the best man was needed for a job, we all looked at Dan, who'd smile as if he were being presented a great gift. He usually said something like, 'Your Highness, I know I've always come in second to you, but if you give me this chance, I know I will prove to you that I am equal to the task.' Our friends would all laugh and the messenger always left confused."

I laughed but quickly stopped. "I'm sorry."

"Don't be. Dan deserved it and so did I for going along with one of his crazy ideas. I couldn't be mad at him for that. He was my best friend."

"He sounds great. I wish I could remember him." I closed my eyes hoping, but nothing.

James whisked my hair behind my ear. "Don't worry, you will."

We silently watched as the sun turned the clouds a bright orange and then pink. I turned my eyes away from the sky and took him in, from the slight stubble appearing on his chin to his hand holding mine. I looked back at his face to find his eyes were sad.

"You miss him, don't you?"

"Yes, but I am more worried for him." He paused, "Afraid I will never see him again."

I knew I should feel the same way, but I didn't. That made me sad, then mad. How dare Manic take my brother away from me! I should be worried for him. I should be missing him. But I hardly knew who he was.

We both leaned against the battlement, I was simmering and he was pondering. Lost in our own thoughts, we watched as the sun disappeared behind the distant mountains.

"We had better head back, Lady A."

"I suppose so," I said, still staring out at the city. Where little specks of light were appearing from lanterns being lit.

"Something worrying you?" he asked.

"I was thinking about all of the horrible things that have happened—there is one tiny good thing in the mix of all the bad."

"And what is that?"

"I got to meet you. I know I could easily be wrong, but I have the feeling that meeting you might not have happened if you and Dan had not chosen to try and capture Manic the way that you did."

"No, I would have found a way to meet you."

"And would I have let you?"

"I'd like to think so," he said, bringing my hand up to his lips. He gently placed a kiss to my fingers. My heart started racing as our eyes connected, and he took a step closer.

"Get down!" yelled Richard.

James threw his arms around me and pulled me down onto the stone walkway. A ping from an arrow string reverberated in my ears even as shouting replaced the sound. An image flashed in my mind of an arrow in the trees, but I didn't get to dwell on it.

"James, get her out of here, now!" Richard shouted.

James pulled us up into a half crouch and Egan joined us on my other side. They both took an arm and we ran along the wall, into the tower, and down the winding steps.

"Are you hurt?" he asked, as we raced toward the castle.

"No. Are you?"

"No," he slowed to a jog and looked back toward the gates and all the commotion.

Through the chaos I heard Richard yell, "Catch him, don't let him get away."

I could see the struggle in James' face. I knew he wanted to be over there catching the bad guy, but he also wanted to stay with me. I looked down at our clasped hands and slowly let out my own breath.

"Go, James," I said, letting go of his hand. He turned slightly confused eyes toward me, and I gestured toward the gates. "Go. I am out of harm's way. Egan will take me inside. I know you want to find out what is going on, so go."

"Are you sure?"

"Yes."

He looked at Egan who nodded in agreement. James quickly kissed me on the cheek, causing a zinging sensation through me, before he darted away. I touched my cheek where his lips had been for a brief moment, holding the sensation there. I knew I should have been trembling in fear, but instead I felt all warm and fluttery.

Egan and I silently hurried inside, but at my door he paused before he opened it for me. "I hope you won't mind me saying so, My Lady, but most women wouldn't have let him out of their sight after something like that. They would have forced him to stay with them."

I smiled, "Is there a compliment hidden in there?"

"There is, My Lady," he said as he pushed my door open and made sure no one was inside. "You are not like most ladies, and the prince is lucky."

He bowed to me and returned to his post a few feet away from my door. I was honored at the bow but also confused. Weren't those reserved for royalty alone?

Chapter 17

~Lady A~

I sat in the window seat of the library and stared out at the rain plunking against the window. It had been four days since the attack on the castle wall. James and the king had interrogated the black-cloaked man more than once, but he wouldn't give up any information. He would laugh or grunt, but that was pretty much it.

I looked out the window at the soggy ground and sighed. I had begged James to let me see him, and finally yesterday afternoon he relented. I walked as close to his cell in the dungeon as I dared. James walked with me, his hand on my shoulder. When the man looked up and saw me standing there, he began laughing like in my dream, except he wasn't the orange-haired monster. He was a mousey-haired, dirty man with stringy hair and missing teeth.

"It's the lady," he said.

"You know who I am?" I asked.

"Yeah, but you sure don't. And that's a good thing miss or else Master Manic would have already slit your throat."

"Don't you dare talk to her like that!" shouted James.

The man stood up to his full height, which wasn't that high. "It's true," he spat. "Mark my words, the moment she remembers anything—she is dead. Unless they get to her before that."

"What do you mean?" I blurted.

"I'll keep it simple. Manic hasn't forgotten you, My Lady. In fact, you are at the top of his to-do list."

"Come on, Lady A, let's go," said James pulling me back, but I couldn't get my feet to move.

"He's coming for me?"

"He already is on his way," he spat, saliva landing on his chin. "You won't last more than a day." He laughed, "You'd be dead now if I hadn't failed."

James pulled me out after that, but the prisoner's words continued to haunt me. I racked my brain after that trying to get the memories to come back. Not to speed up my apparently scheduled demise but to try and stop it—to beat Manic. To finish this!

I had tried every one of Iree's suggestions after that, but nothing had worked. No more flashes that felt like memory. No more familiar things. It was like the black-cloaked man had implanted a stop into my mind, and I didn't like it at all. I needed to do something, but what more could I do? It was infuriating.

I looked back out at the dark clouds and clutched the spine of the book I was reading until my knuckles turned white. I knew I had to be patient, but it was getting harder and harder to do.

I set the book down. I pulled my thin shawl tighter around my shoulders. It was a little chilly in the window seat, but I didn't want to move. I knew more than anyone that I needed to keep trying to spark my memories. I simply couldn't handle it any more today. I knew Iree would be disappointed when she couldn't find me. I, however, needed a break. At least until my uneasiness settled down. So even though it was a little cold I was determined to hide in the library as long as possible.

I jumped when I heard footsteps approaching me. I looked up to find it was only Roland. He smirked at me from behind the bookshelf by my window.

He held up a tiny, blue book. "Good afternoon, My Lady."

"Hello, Roland."

"It looks like the rain has driven us all inside today."

"Indeed, it does," I said adjusting the blanket around my feet.

"I see you like to read, too."

I glanced down at the book sitting next to me and nodded. "Yes, I do." A truth I'm glad I knew.

I looked up to ask what he liked to read to find Roland standing right in front of me, much closer than was necessary. He smiled again. "And what does the lady like to read?" he asked as he leaned down and picked up the book. His face was only inches from mine, and I caught a whiff of what smelled like sweat and firewood smoke.

I felt my skin begin to prickle.

164

I looked past him but couldn't see anyone else in the library. No other movement. The library was extremely quiet. He straightened up and flipped through my book.

"You really should try something more daring, My Lady. I wager you would like it," he said, tossing the book back on the window seat.

"Thank you, I will remember that," I said. Struck with the sudden need to get out of there, I picked up my book and pushed past him. He reached out a hand and placed it on my shoulder before I had taken more than a few steps.

"Don't leave on my account."

"It is getting cold in here. I thought I would go read in my room by the fire," I said as I turned to try and walk away again. But Roland snaked his arm through mine. I tried to remind myself that he was safe. He was friends with James, but something did not feel right.

"Do allow me to escort you."

"That really isn't necessary, Roland." I tried to pull away but he held firm.

"But it is. The rules of chivalry and all," he smirked as if he had some private joke playing through his mind. I felt my stomach clench, and I knew I didn't want to be near him for another second. But I didn't know what to say.

I need a plan, I thought.

Maybe if I let him escort me just to the library door I could come up with some excuse by then. I looked around for something—anything that could get me out of this. But even the old bookkeeper wasn't around.

We were only a few feet from the door when I saw my body guard Egan slumped on the floor. A bloody wound ran along his forehead into his white blond hair. "Egan," I mouthed my voice gone.

Roland whistled and from the shadows two dark shapes emerged. They swaggered slowly toward us, and I felt my heart begin to beat in earnest. They stopped a few feet from us, one on each side, and stood with their arms folded, staring at me from under their dark hoods. Their faces were covered in shadow so I couldn't make out any features but the dullest outline of sneering lips.

On their left shoulder was a red patch, a sword stabbing a crown. The images from my nightmares filled my mind, and I felt my throat constrict. My knees buckled, if Roland hadn't been holding me up, I would have fallen.

"All alone?" laughed the man as Roland shoved me into the nearest chair. His mouth curled up into a devilish smile as he went to stand beside the man who had spoken. I gulped. I yelled internally at myself to run, but my legs were not obeying.

"I had the library cleared out just for you," Roland said, his sickening smile growing wider.

The hooded man who had remained silent so far pulled out from his cloak a short thick stick with a leather wrapped handle. On the end was a ball with metal spikes sticking out of it at all angles like a frazzled porcupine.

I opened my mouth to scream, but Roland stepped forward and covered my mouth with his large, moist hand. The man with the weapon swung it around casually, but I could see what pain it was capable of inflicting.

"When we heard you were still alive, Master Manic was very upset," said the man with the deadly weapon.

"Very upset indeed!" chuckled Roland pushing me back further into the chair. "We were expecting the river to finish you off. He was glad to hear though that you couldn't remember anything and hadn't shared any of our secrets—that is until you gave the prince a perfect description of him. That had him worried you'd soon remember more. He said to take you out. The oaf they sent before failed, and so I had to step in."

"You had to? You are …" I gasped.

"Working for Manic? Yes. And all you fools had no idea."

The two-cloaked men closed in. I started to struggle against Roland's hand, but he held tight pressing my head against the back of the chair.

"Would you like to meet my mace?" asked the cloaked man on my left as he stroked the weapon like it was a baby kitten. "It's my favorite thing in the world," he said as he raised it over his head.

"Too bad you have to die, Lady A. A real beauty like you," said Roland in my ear before he yanked me to my knees on the floor. I cringed into a ball as the mace was raised higher.

"Lady A!" came a shout. In the next moment, Richard sped into the room and tackled the man with the mace. The prince jumped over me and raced after the other cloaked figure that had taken off down a row of books. Edgar followed James but chased after Roland who had taken off down the center isle of books.

I crawled away toward the wall and came face to face with the mace that had fallen to the ground. I yelped and moved further away from it. My eyes kept darting between the mace and the fight. On impulse I reached out and dragged the deadly weapon with me. I scooted until I was behind a chair next to the doors near Egan's limp form. I touched his face, and he let out a slight moan. Satisfied he was alive, I turned back to the fight.

Richard was in a fistfight with the cloaked figure that had held the mace. Prince James was sword fighting the other cloaked man. Edgar had Roland in a choke hold.

I watched as Roland reached down into his boot and pulled out a silver dagger. "Edgar, watch out!" I yelled, but I was too late. Edgar crumpled to the floor and Roland leaned forward breathing hard. He straightened up and didn't even look behind him at one of the men he had claimed was his friend. His eyes burned into my skin as he took a few steps toward me. I knew his mission was to see me dead, and it seemed he wasn't willing to give up on that.

I dragged the mace, around and hefted it up in front of myself. Roland laughed. "A pretty thing like you doesn't know how to use a deadly thing like that."

"No, but I do," shouted James as he came racing out of the bookshelves. His sword had a red stain on it and no cloaked man followed him. He threw himself at Roland and they both stumbled back a few feet. I dropped the mace back to the floor as James pinned Roland against a bookshelf.

"You are a traitor, Roland!" James barked, but I could see the pain behind the anger in his eyes.

"Only in your opinion, James," he said, shoving James away from himself.

"It's a good thing Dan and I never confided in you."

"That's right, or I would have ratted on him and his sister," Roland spat.

I gasped and James clenched his teeth. "How could you, Roland?" James asked, raising his sword. Roland drew his as well and they stood with swords at the ready. "You were a Knight of Salvina. A man of honor. You were my friend. I trusted you."

"'Were' being the truest word you have ever spoken. You and I *were* the best of friends when we were children, until Daniel started showing me up in the practice fields. Then all you cared about was him. What did Dan like to do? What was Dan's opinion? Let's wait to do anything interesting until Dan arrived." Roland swung his sword high over his head.

"What are you talking about?" James bellowed as he blocked Roland's strike.

"Yeah, Edgar, Frederick, and Darwin didn't seem to care, but I did. Manic offered me much more than you ever did, James." A hate stronger than I had ever seen emerged on Roland's face as he fought against James. James stumbled back from Roland's angry strikes but recovered in time to block a deathblow.

"Now you'll never do anything fun again. Manic will win and Dan is dead."

James froze with his sword still raised, and Roland grinned, panting. "Yeah, that's right. Manic killed him when he realized that he was a fake trying to learn our secrets. I told Manic I knew he was a good-for-nothing spy, and should be killed as an example. Manic agreed. Dan's gone, James. Dead."

"No."

"Yes."

"I won't believe that."

"Then you are a fool. Manic wasn't gong to let him live. He doesn't accept betrayal. I saw Dan's dead body myself lying in the dirt."

James stood there breathing hard, but I could see the heartbreak in his eyes. Dan was his best friend. Dan was my brother. Coldness settled in my chest.

"Manic is a true friend, James. He keeps his promises. Unlike you." Roland attacked James, but he blocked again.

"Manic is a traitor and liar, Roland," James said as he parried again and again.

"He's always kept his word to me."

"Only until he no longer needs you," argued James. He pushed Roland to the floor. Roland rolled away but stopped moving when James sword tip touched his chest.

"That's not true," Roland seethed, his eyes smoldering toward James.

"It is true and you know it. Somewhere deep down you know it is the truth."

A shout sounded from the library doors as more guards came running into the room. They dragged Roland away from James kicking and punching but three guards finally restrained him. Three more guards came and removed Richard's man as well.

"You will regret this, James," Roland spat as he was being lugged out. "You have now given Manic more reason to attack the castle. He will come after us sooner than you think, like a true friend."

"No, he won't," James said, turning to look at his 'friend' one last time. "All he cares about is himself. He won't give you a second thought when he learns you are in prison. And if he happens to see you again, he will kill you for failing him."

"No, he won't, you will see."

"Lock him up," James muttered, looking away from Roland.

"You will be sorry for this, James!" Roland yelled.

James watched until the traitors were dragged out the door. He turned to me after Roland's shouts faded away.

"Are you hurt at all?" he asked.

I shook my head. I wasn't hurt. I felt numb.

"There is still hope for Dan."

I nodded not trusting my voice. I wasn't sure where he was getting his hope from, but I wished I could borrow some.

His jaw tightened as he walked over to Edgar who was lying a few feet away. James bent down and touched his neck. Richard went and stood next to James. James shook his head and Richard's shoulders slumped. Edgar was gone. I felt tears well up in my eyes, but I blinked them back.

A few more guards came in and dragged the other cloaked man out of the library, but they carefully picked up Edgar and respectfully carried him out. Egan was roused next.

"I'm sorry," he said the moment his eyes opened. "They ambushed me; I didn't have a chance …"

"It's all right Egan. I am fine." I said.

"I'll do better I promise. I know I can do better."

I could only nod but that seemed to be enough reassurance for him as he limped away with the guards.

James, Richard, and I stayed frozen to our spots until everyone else had left. I couldn't have moved if they had asked me to. Finally, after the room was quiet again, James seemed to unfreeze and he came to me.

"Are you sure you are not hurt?" he asked holding out his hand. His eyes looking me up and down.

I shook my head and didn't move to take his hand. James didn't force me up; instead he sat down behind the chair with me.

"Look at me, Lady A." James gently placed his hands on my jaw and tipped my face up. I found myself staring into his light blue eyes. With his face only inches from my own I could see hidden tears in his eyes. I wasn't surprised. Edgar and Roland had been his friends. I made my heavy feeling arm move and softly touched his face. I tried to smile, but he didn't. He closed his eyes and leaned into my hand.

"I am sorry, Lady A, if I had known."

"This was not your fault, James. You had no reason to suspect him any more than anyone else," I said, pulling back my hand. He let me go as well. We both sat with our backs against the wall. I felt tears running down my face, but I didn't do anything to stop them. I wasn't sure why I was crying. I think somewhere deep inside I knew. And it had to do with Dan.

Richard stood a little way off faithfully guarding us as the castle was searched for any more intruders. We didn't say anything for a long time. Finally, when my tears stopped flowing, I spoke up.

"Will your family be safe?"

"They will be fine. I am sure they are all locked in their rooms with five or so guards each," he said.

"Thank you for rescuing me," both of you," I whispered, my eyes flickering to Richard.

James let out one short laugh, "It was luck really. Good timing. I wish I had realized Roland was the traitor. The way he was looking at you in court the other day should have tipped me off. It was as if you were a piece of nicely seasoned meat, he couldn't wait to sink his teeth into."

"You thought that, too? I didn't know you were watching him."

"I was watching you," he said taking my hand.

"I should apologize, James. I know I brought this on. If not for me, and my memory loss, Edgar would be …"

"No this was all Roland's fault. He did this. Not you."

"But if I could only remember …"

"You can not blame yourself for that either, Lady A. None of this was your fault. I should have listened to you. You were never wrong before. You always kept Dan out of the worst trouble. We should have heeded you. And I should have realized Roland wasn't acting normal—that he was acting like a traitor."

"How do we know if that isn't also true of Dan or me?" I said voicing the fear I had hardly acknowledged since the king confronted me when we arrived.

"No, don't even think such things. You and Dan are the last people who would betray us, of that I am sure."

"Think about how Roland tricked you. What if we did, too? Roland probably knew about Dan at some point. What if Dan knew about him but didn't tell us?"

"There is no chance of that."

"How do you know that for sure, James." I stood, my blood suddenly on fire.

"Apparently we have never met face to face until now. I could be anyone." I jabbed my thumb to my chest. "I could be part of some evil plot like Richard originally thought, and not even know it. How can you claim to know me so well when I don't even know myself?"

I turned and darted through the door. I started down the hall, but he followed me.

I brushed angry tears off of my cheeks and refused to look at him.

"Lady A, stop," he said grabbing my arm. I paused but didn't turn to face him. "We wrote letters, Lady A, for the last two years. I do know you."

"What could a letter really tell you about me, anyway? I could have written anything in a letter. I could have lied, I could have …"

"I know for sure that you are not part of Manic's plots. You are not a traitor."

I threw my hands into the air and stormed away. "We know nothing about me for sure except that I am the ambassador's daughter. I am called Lady A and I have a weird obsession with braiding my hair."

"We know more than that."

"Not much more."

"You may not, but I do. I know much more than that," he said reaching for my hand. I pulled it away.

"Do you? I could have been told to write to you, *Hello, prince, It's me again. Keep my brother out of trouble, will you? By the way we are plotting against you, but don't worry. The end!*" I shouted as I took off down the hall again.

James grabbed my shoulder and pulled me to a stop. His face was hard. "It wasn't like that, Lady A. You are no villain. I know it as sure as I know my feet are on the floor. I have been dying to meet you for over a year. Your letters enticed me, intrigued me so much that I could hardly find any sort of interest in any other girl. And I expected that when we did meet you would feel the same way, too."

He drug his hand through his hair, "But instead, you don't remember anything at all. Because of Manic, I am stuck still trying to meet the girl who …" he stopped there his hands clenching and unclenching.

"Come on," he grabbed my hand and pulled me through the halls with Richard at our heels. He stopped a floor up at a pair of large oak doors, let go of me, and sped inside. I looked at Richard who only shrugged.

He came back with an ivory box in his hands. "Richard, escort her to her room and make sure there is more than Egan alone to guard her." He thrust the box at me. "You want proof that you are not a villain, here you go. Learn who you are, and see for yourself." He slammed his door a little harder than I thought was necessary.

I stared at the door, the anger instantly draining out of me. I looked at Richard and he held out his arm to lead me away.

"Will he be all right?" I asked.

"I'm sure he will," said Richard with a smile that I felt was hiding a laugh. I didn't find anything funny with our conversation. "It's been a hard afternoon, but he will be fine."

He bowed at my door and nodded to the three guards standing there. Egan had a bandage on his head but a determined stance and a smile on his face.

Netta was inside, my room all frantic, but I told her I was fine. All I needed was rest. She readily agreed and left me alone. I walked to my fireplace and found where the light was best. I sat down and closed my eyes. Forcing my blood to stop racing. A few minutes later I felt calm enough to open James's box. Inside were letters.

Lots of letters.

Chapter 18

~Lady A~

I quickly flipped through the letters and realized the same person had written them all. Dates had been scrawled across the tops of most of them. I decided to start with the oldest one in the bunch.

Dear Prince James,

My brother is Daniel Albon, your best friend. I am his sister and very afraid for him. As I am sure you realize, he has a very adventurous sprit and often gets into trouble. I don't mind him having adventures, in fact I love to hear about them, but I fear that he has gotten in over his head this time with his battle of arms plot.

When he mostly lived at home with us, I could stop him from his more dangerous ideas, but he is usually in Saris now with you. Involved heavily in his training. Which by the way, I also support. But I need you to do me a favor. He won't listen to me this time. He thinks with his latest training that he can do much

more than is safe. I wonder if you will add your voice
to mine to help me stop his crazy scheme?
Respectfully,
Lady A

I wasn't sure what to think, except that I really must care a lot
about my brother. Enough to write the prince. I doubted someone
working for Manic would have said the things I did in this letter. So,
I pushed that particular worry to the back of my mind for now and
made a mental note: I like my brother. I unfolded the next letter.

Dear Prince James,
    Forgive me for signing my name
unconventionally, but I think I will let you wonder at
this mystery. You shall have to guess my name if you
truly wish to know it for, I am not inclined to tell you.
I am holding my name back because I want you to
write to me again, as you will need to if you are to
help me keep Dan out of trouble. I expect your first
guess in your next letter.
Cheerfully,
Lady A

I laughed. I guess I really was a tease. Deciding it would be a
benefit to write some of this down, I raced to the desk and pulled out
some parchment, a quill, and ink. I took them all back to the fire and

wrote: *Lady A is 1. Someone who cares about her brother. 2. A tease: she has a sense of humor.* I compared my writing with the letters just in case. I couldn't help my grin when I saw that they matched. I was glad; I wanted this all to be true. With that done I opened the next letter and eagerly read.

> Dear Prince James,
>
> No, No, No, I'm not giving hints. You shall have to wonder if the A stands for my last or first name. It adds to the fun don't you think? No, both of your guesses were wrong. It isn't Charlotte or Adele. I told Dan capturing gypsies was not that adventurous, and he seems to be placated by both of our disapprovals. Apparently, we make a great team in ruining all of his fun! I am glad we agree that sometimes he needs fewer adventures!
> Sincerely,
> Lady A

I giggled at my own wit and quickly scanned through a few more letters—each one making my smile grow. I gathered I was *3. a cheerful person* because my letters seemed to be so lighthearted. However, I was frowning a few letters later.

> Dear Prince James,

No, I will not be joining my brother at court. Nice try though with the formal invite you enclosed. I am sorry to tell you that I have vowed to never go to court again. And it is a vow I intend to keep. The one and only time I went was a complete disaster. One that I never wish to relive. Besides, I know that your real reasoning for the invitation is to find out my name. I am sorry to tell you that your plan has failed. But I wish you a wonderful time. And no, my name is not Alice.

Your friend,

Lady A

Friend? That was the first time I had written that word in the letters. I wrote it down: *4. friend of the prince*. I knew it was I who penned the word, but I couldn't help finally and wholeheartedly believing that it was true.

Dear James,

I am sorry that I did not attend Dan's knighting. I am very proud of him, and I am not as selfish as you claimed me to be. I actually was going to brave the journey and come to court, despite my anxieties, for his special day. But I fell ill a few days before. So ill that I could hardly move. The sickness has yet to leave me completely. According to the town healer, I shouldn't be feeling even close to myself for another week or more. I understand your anger, but it was not my fears that kept me away. I feel bad that I missed it, but it could not be helped. I couldn't be happier for him. I am not offended by your chastising letter, but please know that I am not a terrible sister. Please know, that I didn't mean to cause hurt for either of you.

By the way, my name is not "Selfish Beatrix" as you guessed.

Genuinely,

Lady A

I found myself wishing for the letter he had sent me, simply to compare my words with his. The James I knew seemed to be in control pretty much always; it would have been interesting to know what he was like when he was truly angry. I looked at the ivory box. Could I possibly have his letters at my home in a box like this? I was beginning to hope so.

Dear James,

Annie and Hannah are both wrong. Who said that you could keep guessing more than one name per letter? Hmm? And I do forgive you. Like I said, I understand why you were angry. Think nothing more of it. It's over and done with now. Upon further reflection I have decided that telling you my favorite flower wouldn't help you in the slightest to guess my name. It is a primrose. I know it's not exotic or anything close to what you have growing in your exquisite gardens, but I love them, with their little star-like centers and little heart-shaped petals.

Your Friend,

Lady A

"Oh," I said. At Iree's tea, James had brought me a primrose. This was how he knew. It did seem a little unfair that he knew so much about me, and at the moment I knew so much less about him.

I read through a few more letters and noticed how I, and I assumed James, started signing the letters differently. After "your friend" there was "sincerely yours." Then "yours truly," and then just "yours."

I hesitated writing down my next thought, but I had committed to this. I took a deep breath and wrote on my paper, *5. we were falling in love.* I watched the ink slowly dry for a few moments, the tip of the "e" being the last part to dry. I wanted to think about that fact longer, but the unread letters were pulling my attention away. I wanted to keep learning more.

I read a few more letters before one near the bottom of the stack caught my eye. It looked more crumpled than the rest and the creases made it look like it had been opened and read multiple times.

I read it slowly more than once. I thought it would get better after the second reading, but it didn't. My muscles tensed even more with the third reading.

My Dear James,

I have become aware that you are choosing to trust my brother, Dan, with the most dangerous, foolish, and, riskiest plan that I have ever heard of— worse than anything he has wanted to do before.

Please don't do this. I beg you, James. There has to be another way to stop Manic. You and I usually agree on things, and we both have been able to talk Dan out of some of his crazy ideas. Why, I must know, on the most perilous of notions do we disagree? Why didn't you stop him, James? I tried to stop him myself when he came to tell me, but he wouldn't listen to me. James, please tell him not to do this. Throw him in the dungeon if you must, but stop him. I am most desperately begging you! Please, James, he could die.

Most anxiously,

Your Lady A

Now I understood why James kept saying Dan's disappearance was his fault. He had not stopped Dan from his crazy plan to spy on Manic, and it had led to all of us getting hurt. I thought about Roland boasting about how Dan was dead and I felt a shiver prickle all over my skin. *Could I have stopped Dan?* I wondered. *Did I try hard enough? And if I had been successful would he be alive today?* I so hoped Roland was lying about my brother's death, but I doubted it.

With my thoughts churning faster, my mind fuller than it had been in days, I decided to call it a night. I stretched and was about to put the box away when I noticed another piece of parchment in the box. It wasn't folded and also wasn't written in my hand. Curious, I slowly pulled it out and saw that this one was addressed to me. For some reason my heart began pounding faster again. I took a few deep breaths to clear my head and read James' letter.

> My Dearest Lady A,
>
> I am more than tortured today. Though I will not send this letter I have to write it. I was informed this morning by my mother that it is time for me to start looking for a wife. She says that the only reason they have let me put it off this long is because of Manic. She said we couldn't put it off forever and that I had better start actually looking.
>
> At court today, I tried to put in order the girls that I found the most interesting. But you ended up at the top of the list. I haven't even seen your face or talked to you in person. We have only ever written letters so how could you be at the top of my list? But you are!

At dinner my mother wanted a report, of course. And when asked if any of the ladies intrigued me enough to pursue, I had to shrug. I don't know if she would understand that my answer to her question was you. You, my Lady A, intrigue me like no other lady ever has, and I don't see a promise of meeting you anytime soon. I am tortured because you will not allow me to come see you in Veyon, and you refuse to come to Saris.

I might have a little time to stall, however. As much as they would like me to get married, they want me to stop Manic more. So that is still my priority. Dan and I have the beginnings of an idea that I know you will not like. I hope you will one day forgive me for that when our plan is successful and we are freed from Manic. I wish though that we could meet with you. I want to talk this plan through with you and Dan together in the same room—the argument off paper.

I want to put a face to the woman who intrigues me the most. I know you won't see this letter, but know that you are still tormenting me and I love it as much as I hate it. Lady A, I love the you I know so far, and I want to know you better.
As soon as I can.
Always yours,
James

I nearly crumpled the paper as warm flutters moved up my arms. I had no idea that James was *that* much in love with me. I wasn't sure if he had meant for me to read this last letter, but I held it to my chest until my heartbeat returned to normal. I had to do something. I was done being "poor Lady A who lost her memory." I looked down at my list. I wanted to be this girl—the girl that James loved. I cared deeply for him too, probably more then I now knew.

I looked at the pile of letters and an idea came to me. It felt as if it had always been waiting there waving a bright red flag, and I had been too lost to see it. Veyon. I needed to go home. That thought scared me more than I wanted to admit, but the moment I thought about it I knew it was the right course of action. I needed a trigger to get myself back, and there was no better place for that than my own home.

I scooped all the letters up and carefully placed them in the box. I hesitated putting in James's letter. I wanted to keep it, but I tucked it under the rest just in case he had not intended for me to read it. I looked at my mirror and straightened my dress. *You can do this, Lady A, be brave.* I marched to the door making all three of my guards jump.

"Egan, please lead me to Prince James's room," I said with as much authority as I could muster. He bowed and led the way. A few minutes later, I knocked on the oak doors to his room. Richard and Egan stood whispering quietly behind me. The whispers were probably about me, but I held my chin firm and would not be intimidated.

James answered the door. His shirt was un-tucked and his vest was missing. His eyes rose, and he hastily tucked in his shirt.

"Lady A, is everything all right?"

"James, I need you to do something for me tomorrow morning," I said quickly. I couldn't do with any small talk, I had to get this out before I lost my nerve.

"What is it?"

"I need you to take me to Veyon."

"Why?" he asked his eyes narrowing.

"I need to get my memories back, and I think my home is the answer."

"No, Lady A, it is too dangerous. I'm sorry. I will not risk your life."

"It is the only thing we haven't tried. If I were able to look at my room or the garden I played in, my memories would come back. I know it. And I want them to, even if I have to remember some of the scary things." I held out the box and he took it. "I want to be that girl again, James. I want to be more than who I am right now. You can take as many guards with us as you want."

"No. It is not worth your life. Your memory will come back eventually. It has started already."

"But not fast enough for me or the kingdom. I need to remember. Now"

He sighed, "Lady A, Manic is probably waiting for us to make that mistake. Roland said he wants you dead, probably now more than ever."

"James, please..."

"No!"

"What was the point of reading those letters then?" I said clenching my fists.

"I wanted you to know who you were, and that there was no way you were working for Manic. You know that, now—right?"

"Yes, I do. But can no longer wait calmly for my memories to return. I must act. I must remember." I touched the ivory box. "I need to be her again. I think it will be my home that does it."

"I can't, Lady A. Not now when we know how much Manic wants your head. Not now when he will be so angry at Roland's failure."

I felt my heart sink until it felt like it was squishing my stomach. I was hurt by his refusal, but I wasn't about to be stopped. The bravery and joy I had felt earlier molded into something new—something fiery, powerful, and determined. "Fine." I marched away with Egan following behind me.

"I'm sorry," he called, but I didn't turn around.

If he was unwilling to help me then I would find my own way home. I would crawl there if I had to. I had to go, and I would not be swayed. I stormed into my room and tore open my wardrobe. I pulled out boots and the warmest cloak I could find. I was going to get my memories back right now. I was done waiting. And honestly so was the kingdom.

Chapter 19

~James~

I watched Lady A storm off, but I knew I was doing what was best—what was safe. She would see that I was right eventually. I looked at Richard who was glaring at me.

"What?"

"She's right, James. I think she should go."

"Are you betraying me now, too?" I shouted, my frustration hitting the top of my limit.

"No, only stating my opinion."

"Thanks," I said. "How about you take your opinions and get out of here. Go check on the patrols."

I closed my door with a snap.

I couldn't believe Richard was taking her side. How dare he! He was supposed to agree with me. He was supposed to be on my side. Always!

I stomped across my room and tossed the ivory box into my wardrobe. I knew they were both angry with me and probably had every right to be. I was as sure as she was that going home was exactly what she needed to trigger her memory. But I was not willing to sacrifice her life for her memories. She had to understand that. Richard had to understand that. I was doing what was best.

I wasn't absolutely sure what I wanted her to gain from her letters. Her memory back? Her undying love for me? No, I wanted her convinced that she was not a traitor. I wanted her to believe that she was a good person, and see the girl who I had wanted to fully fall in love with. To see why I was so much in love with her now.

A pounding on my door jolted me out of my thoughts. I almost ignored it. I really didn't want to face Richard right now even for a simple report on the patrols.

The pounding began again and I yelled, "Come in already."

A servant opened the door and quickly bowed. "Prince James, the king wishes to see you. He has news on Manic."

"Manic?!"

"Yes, Sire."

I darted to the door. "Well, come on." We raced into the hall, and I noted Richard's absence. I felt a little bad for yelling at him, but I needed people to be on my side right now and not adding to the defiance I was experiencing.

The servant and I charged full speed down the hall. Frederick caught up to us before we had gone too far. "What's going on, James?"

"Father has received word about Manic."

He smirked and fell into step behind me. "Great. Does that mean we all get to go casual this evening?"

I glanced down at my slightly disheveled appearance and glared at him. "I think I will be forgiven."

"No doubt."

He put an arm on my shoulder and pulled me to a stop. "James, are you doing all right? I know Roland's betrayal and Edgar's death hit me hard enough. I can't imagine how …"

"I will be fine, Frederick. We all will. Do me a favor will you?"

"Sure."

"Find Richard for me."

I could see questions in his eyes, but he held them in and nodded, for which I was grateful. I might be angry with Richard, but if we had news on Manic, I knew I needed him by my side.

I darted into my father's chambers without knocking and found him getting dressed in full armor. "Father, what's happening?"

My father waved his servant over who presented him three different sword options. "We are going to war, Son." He lifted each one, but selected the first.

"Father, whom are we going to war with?"

"Manic's riders have been spotted in Avern. And not only a small group like before. It looks like Manic is gathering his army together. He himself has been sighted. He plans to take Avern and

Saris next. I will not allow him to do this. I am taking half of the army with me, and we will defeat him."

"I will get ready myself to accompany you," I said turning toward the door.

"No, son. I must do this. I must bring Manic to his knees. I need you to remain here with the other half of the army in the odd chance that we fail. I need to know that you are protecting our home and our family." He came forward and put his hand on my shoulder. "I know I can count on you."

"Of course, you can Father. It's just that I always thought I would be the one leading the troops into battle."

"You've done well, Son, taking the lead thus far. But I must see this done. You've had a hard-enough day. We don't need to add a battle on top of everything else. Tell me that I can count on you, James."

I felt like I had been slapped in the face, but I knew there would be no arguing with him. Not when he was already nearly in full armor. "Yes, Father, you know you can." I bowed and turned to leave.

"James, this is not a punishment for earlier today. But I cannot afford this battle to go any direction but the way I wish."

I stepped forward. "Roland deceived us all. And Edgar died a hero's death."

"That might be true, but my decision is final. There have been far too many mistakes concerning Manic, and I am taking full control. You may go and start your preparations for protecting the castle if it comes to that."

I gritted my teeth and offered a short bow. He turned away and began instructing his servant. I stomped out of the room. This day was getting worse and worse. At least it was finally the evening now. Not much more could happen.

I called for Frederick and Darwin to come to my room to discuss plans. I would show my father that I could take care of the Kingdom. That I was worthy to be king one day. I would show him that I was not some kind of bumbling fool.

*   *   *   *

~Lady A~

I opened my door and three pairs of eyes immediately looked my way. What was I going to do about my guards? After what had happened today, there was no way that they would let me wander off alone. I looked at Egan—his determination still clearly set in his face. Maybe he was so desperate to prove himself he would do anything.

"Egan I … need to go for a walk. I can't stay trapped in this tiny room anymore. Not with everything that has happened today." I felt bad for lying, but I knew if I told him my true reasons, he would have barred my door, and reported me to James. I couldn't risk that.

Besides I really did feel anxious. He nodded and we left my other guards at my door.

We walked close to the castle walls as I tried to think of a way to escape him. A part of me wanted to ask him to take me himself; I didn't want to go alone. But if James had said no, who would say yes?

I had just calculated my chances of racing out of the gates unnoticed as a zero when Richard came out of the guardhouse looking more than a little unhappy. He stopped walking when he caught sight of Egan and I.

He rushed toward us. "What are you doing out here in the dark? It's dangerous."

"I know, Richard, but ..." I glanced behind me and saw Egan was leaning forward (no doubt wondering what all my wandering around was about).

"I can trust you. I know that. I know that James and my brother trust you more than anyone. If I tell you both something in confidence do both of you promise not to get angry or run off and inform the Prince?"

Richard's brows furrowed a bit, but he crossed his arms and nodded. I looked at Egan and he shrugged his shoulders and nodded too.

"I know that it is dangerous, and I understand that Manic wants me dead. But I also know that if I go home, I will get my memories back. I can feel it. I don't care how I get there, but I am leaving right now. I don't care what James said. Please Richard, don't stop me from going."

Richard started to smile, but Egan's jaw dropped open.

"Lady A, you know that you are asking me to betray the prince?"

"Not betray him, I just don't want you to tell him."

"You are determined?" asked Richard. "Are you saying that even if Egan and I dragged you back to your room right now you would only attempt to escape again?"

"Yes. Though I would rather not test my bed sheets," I said, holding my chin as firm as I could. I didn't want to give him any reason to doubt me.

Richard's smile grew. "Allow me to take you myself, My Lady, but only because I believe you have the right to go home if you want too. And you shouldn't go alone."

"Really?"

"But we best hurry." He said his gaze flicking up toward the castle. "We are risking James's anger as it is. Egan?"

He bowed. "I will go with my charge."

I felt tears in my eyes, and threw my arms around them both. "Thank you."

Richard offered me his arm. Egan took my other one and together we raced through the dark to the stables.

*   *   *   *

~James~

Darwin and Frederick arrived in my chambers a few minutes after I called for them. Both looked a little happier than I thought they should. But perhaps that was only because of my current state of mind.

"How did we get the honor to stay here instead of accompanying the king?" teased Darwin as he slumped into a chair, tossing his feet on the table.

"Have the troops left?" I asked.

"Yep, I saw them marching out on my way here," said Darwin.

"It pays to be the prince's friends," said Frederick, sitting down as well and resting his head on his arms. "And not marching off in the dark."

We got right to work. The nice thing about working with my friends was we already knew how each other thought. It took us less than an hour to come up with our plan and the same amount of time for my head to cool.

"I wonder where Richard is with that report," I said, pulling out my armor.

Frederick's eyes narrowed. "When did you send him?" he asked.

"Before I met with my father."

Darwin and Frederick exchanged looks. Frederick shot to his feet and threw opened my door.

"Richard isn't out here."

I debated if I should be worried or angry. I knew I told him to get out of there, but Richard wasn't one not to come back. I pulled my sword off of the table and the three of us ran into the hall.

"Do you think he's in trouble?" asked Darwin as we ran.

"If he is, then everyone in the castle is, too," said Frederick.

I skidded to a halt. "Mother, Lady A, Iree."

"Go check on Lady A, James. We will find the queen and your sister." I nodded and we went our separate directions.

I ran to Lady A's room and the first thing I noticed was the absence of Egan. Her two other guards lay slumped against the wall. I didn't stop to see if they were alive or asleep on the job. I pushed her door open and ran into her room. It appeared to be empty.

My heart started pounding faster. "Lady A? Lady A, are you here?" There was no answer.

I tore out of the room and shook her guards. They both jerked awake and started mumbling excuses. "Quiet. Did someone knock you out?"

"Um … no, we're sorry, Your Highness."

"We will do better we swear. We are worthy of this appointment."

"Stop. Lady A is not in her room."

I expected them to look shocked but they shrugged. "Must not be back yet, Sire."

"Back? Where did she go?"

"We don't know, Your Highness. She came out and said she needed to walk. She told us to wait here but took Egan with her."

I didn't like it. Why would she go walking at night? When it was so dangerous. "Stay at your post and send me word immediately if she returns."

"Yes, Sire!" They said, standing straight and turning their eyes toward her door.

I ran down the hall and found Frederick and my mother racing down the stairs. "James, Iree and I are fine, but Frederick says Richard is missing," said my mother.

I stopped moving. Richard was missing. Lady A was possibly missing. The stink of betrayal filled my senses nearly choking me.

"James, what is it?" asked my mother, putting a hand on my arm.

"Lady A is not in her room. Egan apparently went with her somewhere. And Richard is missing." I looked at Frederick. "Where is Darwin?"

"He went to see if Richard was in the guard house or the barracks."

"I'm sure they are all right, James," said my mother in her usual calm manner.

"After a day like today?" I asked. "How can you be? Manic is apparently in Avern. Roland betrayed us, Edgar is dead, and now people are missing."

Darwin came running into the hall, his sword clanking against his side. "James, you are never going to believe this. Some of the men saw Richard riding out just after the troops left and two other riders were with him. They couldn't be sure, but they swore that one of the riders was a lady."

My fury rose as I realized who the lady rider had to be. "How could she ... How could he ... What is happening today! Everyone is turning their back at me."

I threw my helmet at the ground, the resonating bang echoing down the hall. Didn't they realize how dangerous this was? Didn't they know that they were probably walking right into a trap?

I cursed under my breath and started pacing. My father wanted me to stay here to protect my mother, sister, and kingdom. My father had made that very clear. My place was here. But I had to go after her.

"Frederick could Richard betray me? Could he even for one moment ..."

Fredrick put a hand on my shoulder. "I doubt it, James, I really do. But—I honestly would have said that of any of us only a few days ago."

I hated to think that Richard could betray me, but on the slight chance that could be true I had to do something.

Mother stepped up to me and stood right in front of my face. "Go after her, James."

"Mother, I promised father that I would protect the castle. That I would be here for you and Iree. I can't go. I have a job to do."

"A job I will gladly take on, James," said Frederick. "Darwin and I know the plan. We are prepared for the worst. Go after her."

"Your father said to protect your family. She is family now, if my own observations haven't led me amiss. Go! Bring her back safe," convinced my mother.

I looked from my mother, to Frederick to Darwin, picked my helmet up off the ground and raced out of the castle. I sheathed my sword and made sure my boot dagger was in place, while Drumund saddled my horse.

Who knew what I was about to face? One thing was for certain. If I found out Richard had betrayed me—I'd run him through.

Chapter 20

~Lady A~

We rode through the darkness at a quick pace behind the troops to the city of Avern. But instead of turning into the city we broke off and rode past. Without the wall of horses and flapping capes, I felt some of my resolve falter. Manic would never attack a small army, but three travelers alone on the road were his favorite kind of prey. According to the soldiers Manic was in Avern, so we hoped there was no chance of an attack.

The wind began to blow with the iciness that only the Fall air knew. The earlier clouds had cleared for the time-being and the moon shown brightly lighting up the path ahead of us. I felt bad in a tiny place of my heart for going against James' wishes, but my determination to find myself overrode the guilt.

I kept looking around me hoping for a quick miracle—a sudden whoosh of memories—that would shove the blankness out of my mind. I knew it probably wouldn't happen until I arrived home, but if it happened sooner than later maybe we could return before

James found out we had left. Maybe if I remembered he would be so happy that he wouldn't have us tried for treason.

"We're almost there, Lady A," said Richard a few moments later. I started looking around with renewed vigor at the trees and the houses that were starting to appear.

Nothing came zooming into my mind, and my heart started to ache. What if everything stayed unfamiliar? What if I could never again be the girl in the letters?

I pushed down my fear and rode forward. I couldn't think like that. This had to be my answer.

A few minutes later, a long drive lined with willow trees came into view. I pulled my horse to a stop, sat up straighter, and leaned forward. The men hung back a pace or two. Barely discernible through the tree's dancing leaves was a large, old, stone house. My breath stalled in my throat and my heart began racing simultaneously.

I knew this place.

I kicked my horse into a run, and we galloped down the drive as fast as we could go.

"Lady A?" called Richard, but I could not look back.

"Lady A," shouted Egan as well, but I hardly heard them. I reined my horse in hard when we arrived at the front of the house. I jumped off, grabbed my skirts, stumbled for a few steps, but kept my footing. I took off toward the front door; my heartbeat speeding up with every step.

"Lady A," called Richard again, but I didn't turn.

Tears began to fall down my face as I reached the landing. My feet failed me inches from the door and I fell to my knees. I reached my hand up, touched the door and began to sob.

Images began filling my head. I saw myself as a little girl pacing back and forth in front of this door waiting for my parents to come home. I saw a black cat that I had been chasing around the willow trees. I saw my tears dripping onto a letter, saying my mother wouldn't be home in time to escort me to court.

This was my home.

"Lady A, are you all right?" Richard asked from behind me.

"I live here. This is my house," I croaked, pressing my fingers into my forehead.

"Yes, it is," he said, and I could hear the joy in his voice. I turned to look at him and Egan, not bothered by the tears streaming down my face. I stood and pulled them both into a hug.

"Thank you! I remember. I remember the trees, the house, the willow-lined drive." I closed my eyes as more memories fell back into place and pushed out the muddiness that had lived there far to long.

"We knew you would, My Lady," said Egan. I released them both and saw that Egan was beaming.

"Even though I was so determined to come I was afraid I wouldn't," I said as I whirled around. "That I would never remember any of it."

I reached for the door handle. "Whoa, not so fast," Richard said. I ignored his warning, grabbed his torch and pushed the door open.

I took a few steps into the hall, and gasped when I saw a pool of dried blood on the floor.

"It's not Dan's," Richard said coming in behind me. I let the breath go that I didn't know I was holding.

"Whose is it?" I said barely above a whisper.

"Hewitt's."

The face of our old steward filled my mind, and I swallowed hard. "Oh no. What of the others? What of Mrs. Carlton, and …"

"We don't know, My Lady. We took care of Hewitt, but they were not here when we arrived. We think that they took to hiding."

Egan ran in the room and skidded to a halt. "There is a rider coming full speed down the drive."

We turned and looked back out the door. The rider wore a long cape that flew out behind him.

"It's one of Manic's men," I gasped, backing up into the room. As memories of their terror filled my mind.

"No, I don't think it is, Lady A," said Egan, taking a step back out of the house, his eyes squinted. We watched as the rider rode right up to the house and leapt off of his horse. He flung his hood back and drew out his sword.

It was James.

"Go, go, go!" shouted Richard, pushing me behind him back into the entryway of the house.

"Tell me that you did not betray me, Richard!" James shouted as he climbed the step.

"That you are not leading her into a trap." James shoved Richard against the door and pointed his sword directly at his chest. "Convince me that more than half of my friends are trustworthy," he seethed.

"Whoa, whoa, James," Richard said, sliding his hands up until they were even with his head. Egan took a step forward, but Richard shook his head to stop him.

Richard took a deep breath, his eyes on the point of the sword. "I did not betray you, James. She had a right to come here if she wanted to. She was not a prisoner."

"That is no excuse for going behind my back."

"You wouldn't let her come," argued Richard, lifting his gaze away from the sword. "She was going to go alone if we didn't come with her."

James looked from me, to Richard, to Egan, to his sword point resting on Richards Chest.

Richard kept his hands up above his head, and waited until James too a step back, his sword still raised between them. Richard let his hands fall a fraction. "I would never do you harm, James. You know that. I swore when you were only three that I would always protect you. Tonight, that meant protecting her."

James turned fuming eyes on me. "Do you have any idea what kind of danger there is tonight? Do any of you even know what is happening right now?"

"James," I stepped forward and put a hand on his shoulder. "I remember."

"Great! You should understand why I am so angry with all of you."

"No, James." I said smiling at his confusion. "I remember."

Whatever he was expecting me to say, it obviously wasn't that. He slowly lowered his sword to his side, and took a deep breath. He looked at Richard who smiled.

"Everything?" he asked.

"It's still coming back I am sure, but I remember. And it wasn't Richard's idea. Not any of it. He's right I was going to come alone. He caught me trying to figure out a way to escape, and he knew I wasn't about to give up so, he came to protect me. Egan didn't even know what I was planning until Richard stopped us outside on the grounds."

James looked from me, to Richard, to Egan, again and this time he sheathed his sword. His mouth was still tight, but he no longer looked like a raging wolf defending his den of pups.

Satisfied he wasn't about to kill Richard, I looked toward the stairs. An image of Dan sliding down the banister filled my mind and I smiled.

"Dan. I remember Dan!" I shouted as I darted toward the stairs.

"Lady A?" called James following me.

The good memory turned into a dark one. To the last memory I had of my brother. I gasped.

"He was late, James. Dan was late. The day you were supposed to come for his report." I started running up the stairs two at a time with James behind me and Richard and Egan following us.

"I was so worried. I thought something bad had happened to him." I threw open the door to my sitting room and ran inside.

"What happened?" he asked as I froze, taking in the familiar room.

"Dan finally came bursting into the room. He was wet from the storm." I put a hand to my head as that awful day filled my mind.

I looked toward the window. It was still open and the curtain swayed slightly in the wind. "He made me go out the window, but he stayed in the room."

"Why?' asked Egan from behind me. I turned toward them all a shiver running up my spine.

"He did it to protect me from Manic," I looked at James, and he took a step closer to me. "They were coming to kill me."

"What?!" he said, the last of his anger fleeing his face replaced by a different expression I didn't fully understand.

"It was his last test, James. He was supposed to kill me in order to fully gain Manic's trust. But Dan protected me instead." I felt tears building in my eyes, and I turned away.

"I took Narcissus and rode into the forest, but I heard Dan cry out in pain as I left," I said and spun around to look toward the window. I gasped when I saw a small circle of blood on the floor. It was Dan's blood. I was sure of it.

I stumbled back, but James caught me.

"Dan's dead." I turned in James's arms to look at him in the face. "James, my brother is dead." He pulled me tighter against him held me. I pressed my face to his shoulder and tried to fight the tears.

Dan had sacrificed himself for me. For his country. He had wanted to save us all. But he couldn't save himself.

"I'm so sorry," James said, hugging me tighter.

Suddenly something that Dan had said started doing jumping jacks in my mind, and I pulled away from James and his comfort.

"How many days has it been since that day?" I asked. I looked from James's red eyes to Richard and Egan's.

"Fifteen days. Well, probably sixteen now," answered Richard.

"Oh no. No, you have to all get back to Saris, right now!" I cried shoving James toward the door.

"Why?" asked Egan.

"Manic was planning on attacking the castle tomorrow …
well … today. It was his grand plan. Dan said that today was
special." I rubbed my head trying to remember everything.

"That tomorrow meant something special to Manic.
Something …" I tried to remember all the details, but my mind felt
like it was taking a ride on a spinning wheel.

"Something about today being the day his ancestor lost the
crown … something like that. Anyway, he's been planning to
overthrow the kingdom and the attack on Avern was just to draw the
king out." I looked at James in the eye. "He means to take the
castle."

"Are you sure?" James asked.

"Positive. We knew he was gaining followers, a small army, so
that he could steal the throne. We thought for a while that you could
attack his hideout by Lake Delmar, but he is hardly ever there. He
usually hides out in big, empty houses in the town he wants to attack,
but that was harder to track. Dan tried to find out more about his
plan and this was it."

James stated pacing, but Egan looked confused. "So why
exactly is tomorrow so important to Manic?" Egan asked.

James shook his head. "Because this was the day, years and
years ago, when his great-great-grandfather was forced out of the
kingdom. When, as Manic says, his great-great-grandfather's brother
stole the crown from him."

He started to pace. "Their father didn't like the idea of choosing between his two sons. On his deathbed he told Albert and Arnold to share the kingdom, but Albert—my great-great-grandfather—had to force Arnold out. Arnold had tried to kill Albert in his sleep so he could take the kingdom for himself, and attempted to take his life a couple of times before that."

He paused and turned to face us all. "Manic claims that the history has been recorded wrong. He says Albert wanted the kingdom and he forced Arnold to live out his life in the mines, nearly impoverished, and he never allowed his brother to return to Saris."

"No wonder he says he has a claim to the throne," I said.

"If he even has the blood of Arnold, he still has no claim. He only thinks he does. Arnold was lucky to only have been banished, and not to the mines as Manic claims. Arnold was sent to a manor with servants and everything he could possibly need. It was only when he squandered it all that he started spouting a different story," explained James.

"And passed on his lies to future generations," Richard said his hand on the hilt of his sword.

"Unfortunately," James added taking up his pacing again.

"And now Manic is attacking in mere hours," I said. "While the castle defenses are in Avern."

"Only half of the army followed my father the rest he left to defend the castle." James stopped pacing. "Tree. Mother. They are in the castle. They're in danger."

I gasped; they were in danger because of me. "James, I didn't mean to. I didn't realize."

He put a hand on my shoulder. "This isn't over yet. We still have time to stop this."

"We must tell the king," said Egan. "If we can get the rest of the army back to Saris in time Manic won't stand a chance against us."

"I agree, but more than that we need to protect my family," said James. "We need to leave immediately."

"I'll see if there are rested horses in the stable or yard," said Egan, rushing out.

"I'll help," said Richard, rushing after him.

I fell into a chair, and held my head. My mind was still racing. James walked to the open window and gently closed it. I didn't know what to say to him. I wasn't sure if he was still angry or if he wanted to be left alone.

I looked toward my desk to avoid staring at him. A white piece of parchment caught my eye. I got up and moved to my desk. It was a letter, a letter signed by James.

I gasped and grabbed it as another batch of memories fell into place. A bunch of memories I should have never forgotten.

"What is it?" asked James, coming up behind me. I turned to him with new tears in my eyes and handed him the letter. He looked at it and looked back at me seemingly unimpressed.

"James," I said, taking in his face anew, from his handsome features, to his strong jaw, to his chocolaty hair. "I remember you." I nodded to the letter. "I remember out letters."

A slow smile grew on his face, and he pulled me into a hug. I couldn't believe it. I was hugging James. My James.

Conflicting feelings filled my heart. I remembered my daydreams and my nervousness I had felt about meeting him. I remembered the longing and the pain that I had felt. I remembered my worries that we would probably never be together because of my fears, yet we had been together for over two weeks. We had been together at the castle, a place I had vowed to never go.

I hugged him tighter as my heart realized how much I cared for him and soaked in the feeling of his arms around me.

"So, are you going to put me out of my misery or leave me to feel tortured?" he asked, bringing me out of my swirling thoughts.

I couldn't help the short laugh that escaped me. I pulled away from him until his hands rested on my upper arms. "Whatever do you mean?"

"Torture, I knew it."

I laughed again louder this time. "I have half a mind to let you keep guessing," I said backing up a step.

"Let me?" he said countering my movement by taking a step closer to me. "Don't you mean make me?"

"I couldn't make you do anything," I said.

"I have a few friends who would argue that isn't true."

He offered me his hand, and I took it. "Lady A," he said placing a soft kiss on my hand. "It would be my great honor to learn your name."

I looked down at our clasped hands and for me it felt like the first time he'd held my hand. I had dreamed of this. I suddenly understood why he would have felt so frustrated with me half of the time. "I was scared of you once, did you know?" I said keeping my gaze on our entwined fingers.

James laughed, "Why were you scared of me?"

"Because you were part of a world I feared. It took me days to convince myself to write that first letter to you, but with Dan's life in danger I didn't feel I had a choice. I think I wrote seven or eight letters before the one I sent. I even walked around with it for half a day before I had Hewitt take it to a messenger."

"Was I that scary?"

"No, I was that scared. Ever since my day at court I had a hard time trusting anyone, ever," I laughed. "That's why I signed my name Lady A."

"So, I wouldn't know who you were?"

"No, I knew you'd know I was Dan's sister. It was more that I didn't want to feel like it was really me reaching out. I wasn't one to do that."

"And now?"

"I'm glad I did."

"So?" he said, looking me in the eye.

I sighed as my lips curved into a mischievous smile. "Do you have your list?"

"My what?"

"You know."

His lips twisted like he was trying to fight off a smile of his own. He reached into his jacket just as someone downstairs screamed.

Chapter 21

~James~

My hand instinctively changed direction, and I pulled out my sword instead. "Stay here," I breathed as I slipped out the door. I moved quickly but silently down the stairs. I heard some scuffling and turned into the room to the left of the entrance hall.

Richard was being forced to his knees as they bound his wrists, but Egan lay dead on the floor. "Nice of you to join us, Princey," laughed a man leaning against the fireplace. I took one step forward, but stopped as I felt a sword tip at my back. Two more men moved forward and pointed their swords at my chest.

"Drop it!" the man behind me hissed. I let my sword clatter to the floor.

"Ha ha. Look boys! This boring job has turned out pretty good for us, I'd say. Manic will be pleased," said the man still leaning on the fireplace. He pulled out a small dull-looking dagger and started cleaning his fingernails. "We leave to hunt out some dinner, and fate hands us our salvation. Now where is the girl?"

"What girl?" I spat.

The men laughed, "We know that you wouldn't be here unless the girl wanted to come home. Now, where is she?" I kept my eyes on the floor. "Carter, look upstairs for the lady."

"No," I said knocking the sword tips away from my chest, but before I could turn around the man behind me slammed the hilt of his sword into my shoulder. I fell to the ground. The pain seared through me. They made quick work of tying my hands behind my back.

I heard a scream and the sounds of a struggle. It sounded like she was putting up a good fight. A minute later, Lady A appeared with her hands bound in front of her.

"Don't ever say I don't know how to treat a lady," laughed the man pushing her into the room. He threw her to the ground. His yellow, half-rotten teeth and the stench of death nearly made me retch.

"With this lot, Manic will give us a huge portion of land and maybe even big houses," bragged my captor.

"Throw them in the wagon!" demanded the man by the fireplace as he admired his fingernails. "Don't forget the dead one. Even if he's not breathing, it will show Manic how good we are. Let's get out of this stinking place."

We were all forced to our feet. I watched Richard who nodded to my boot. My dagger. I returned his nod as we were all forced out of the Albon's house and pushed toward a rickety wagon. They tossed Lady A next to the lump that was poor Egan.

Richard was pushed up next, but right as he was lifted up, he made himself fall backwards into me. We crumpled to the ground, but during the confusion and the shouting I felt Richard pull out my dagger. He must have hidden it up the back of his shirt because I didn't see it when he was forced up into the wagon.

I was thrown in last and our captors started arguing about who would ride and who would drive. Richard took advantage of their distraction and began cutting his own ropes.

Richard rolled over to cut my ropes as one of Manic's men climbed up into the wagon seat. We held still while they all settled into place, but as we began moving, they turned their eyes away. Richard cut my ropes quickly, and handed me the dagger. I rolled to Lady A, and cut her free as well.

"Trust us," I whispered in her ear. As the wagon rocked us hard to the left my lips lightly brushed her cheek and I nearly lost my focus.

"One, two, three," breathed Richard. He bolted up, punched our driver in the face, and grabbed the reins. He slapped them across the horse's backs and we jolted forward.

I flung myself over and held onto Lady A and poor Egan so that they wouldn't fall out of the wagon.

We kept a fast pace, but it wasn't long before I heard horses right behind us. "Richard, they are almost on top of us!" I yelled. Richard urged the horses to ride faster, but they were already running at nearly full speed. I knew we wouldn't be able to keep this pace for long. I looked around the wagon. In the corner under the seat was a crossbow.

"Better than nothing," I said. "Hold onto him," I shouted at Lady A indicating Egan. She obeyed, and I reached for the crossbow. Only a few arrows lay in the box beside it. I'd make it work.

I loaded one, turned around, and pulled the trigger. It flew straight and hit its target. I shot another and cursed as the man swerved. I shot my third arrow, and it hit its mark, barely. The man screamed clutching his arm. I shot again and hit another.

Only three of them were left, but I had run out of arrows. They rode up alongside the wagon. One clambered onto the driver's seat in an attempt to take the reins. Richard kicked him off while I threw the crossbow at the other man who was about to jump off his horse into the wagon. Knocked off balance, he fell into the trees and down a small hill. But the other man jumped into the back of the wagon.

He grabbed Lady A and pulled her up. She twisted and elbowed him in the face. He flung his arms back and knocked me over. I fell hard on my arm, against the bottom of the wagon.

I turned in time to see the traitor grab for her again. The wagon went over a bump at the right moment however and she aimed one hard kick at the man. It was well-placed and the last of our captors tumbled out of the wagon and onto the ground.

"Don't slow down too much, Richard. Three of them were left alive, and we don't want them to catch us," I yelled.

"No kidding," he shouted back.

I settled down in the wagon rubbing my arm and smiled at Lady A. "That was one fine kick."

"I was not going to be taken hostage," she said a fire in her eyes I quite liked.

Her eyes suddenly grew wider than a dinner plate. "Oh no, I forgot something."

"You forgot a lot of things, dear," I said tucking her wayward hair behind her ear.

"No, I forgot something that matters right now. Dan told me, when they led your father away from the castle, they would be setting a trap."

"He's going to kill my father?!"

"No, not your father. The trap is for your mother and Iree. James, he wants to take them hostage and ransom the kingdom. He knows your father would give anything up for them. That is why they wanted him out of the castle."

My blood turned cold. *How could I have left them? How could I not have?* I argued back. One thing was for evident. They were certainly in danger.

"Richard, drive faster. We have to get back home to them now!"

Chapter 22

~Lady A~

James and Richard talked about what had to be done as soon as we arrived. I settled down in the wagon as far from Egan's body as I could. I felt my chin quiver when I thought how his death truly was my fault. Memories kept filling my head and I closed my eyes against them. The small headache that had started to form between my eyes didn't help.

Richard kept the horses at a quick pace. I found myself nodding off, but felt bad because I should have been full of nervous energy like them. I was concerned, but I think the return of my memories, the headache and staying up all night was taking its toll. The third time I jerked awake, James scooted closer to me, wrapped his arm around me and gently turned my head to his shoulder.

I lurched awake sometime later as the wagon picked up in speed. I opened my eyes to see our pursuers had finally caught up to us. The city gates were barred when we arrived, but at a signal from

James we were immediately let through. The gates slammed shut behind us and our pursuers were forced to retreat to avoid capture.

The sun had risen by the time we arrived back in Saris, but the thick clouds blowing in obscured the light. Everything was gray. "Any news of the king?" James asked a guard the moment we were inside the city walls and Richard had stopped the wagon.

"Last we heard, Your Highness, was that we were winning the battle in Avern. Our men were driving Manic's men back."

"Excellent. And Manic?"

"Unsure, Sire. No word on him as of yet. "

"Please send a messenger to find out how the king is faring. I need to communicate with him right away. Obtain for me everything we know about Manic's location. I also need an update on the battle immediately."

"Yes, Sire. Right away." James helped me out of the wagon and we all climbed onto fresh horses.

"And take care of him," James nodded to Egan's body in the wagon. "He died a hero. Make sure he is treated as such."

The soldiers nodded and moved into action.

"It seems we made it in time," said James, a lighter note to his voice.

We hurried to the castle and were met by the queen and Iree on the front steps. Guards flanked them.

"You made it back. I was so worried?"

"You were worried. I was worried," James said hugging his mother. "We believe that Manic is going to try and come after you. What are you doing out here?"

"Making sure you were all safe."

Iree ran to me and gave me a huge hug the moment I was on my feet. "Oh, Lady A, I was afraid you were dead. I thought we'd lost you forever!" she cried.

I laughed, "Iree, I'm afraid you are stuck with me."

Her eyes brightened "For forever?"

I glanced over at James and he smiled. "We aren't letting her out of our sight, Iree."

"Good."

"James!" shouted Frederick as he and Darwin ran up to us. "James, Manic has been spotted in Saris."

"What? How did he get past the city gate?" asked James.

"We don't know."

"That can't be good." James turned and looked at us all, and I could feel the tug of war going on inside his head. So did the queen.

"We'll go inside to the safety of our rooms. You need to go son."

James hesitated a moment, his eyes finding mine. "Richard, have extra guards escort them all to their rooms."

Richard nodded, and without another word James left with Frederick and Darwin.

"I hope they find him," I said watching James and his friends run to the guardhouse.

"Before it's too late," added Richard.

"Too late for what?" asked Iree.

Richard and I exchanged looks. But the queen stepped in and saved us from an awkward explanation. "Iree, let's go choose some treats for the kitchens to send up. We don't want to be without anything fun to eat while we wait for this all to end."

"Oh yes, of course," she curtsied to us and bounced away with her mother and their guards.

I went with Richard. "Manic can't get into the castle, can he?" I asked as we walked up the stairs.

Richard shrugged. "It is not impossible. Especially with the amount of people he's turned. But it also won't be easy."

I didn't like the sound of that.

"What can I do, Richard?"

He chuckled lightly. "You, My Lady, can rest. This is almost over."

"How can I?" I asked. Thinking about James looking for Manic worried me to my very core. Manic wouldn't hesitate to kill James. Not for one moment.

"Find a way," he said, escorting me up another flight of stairs.

"What are you going to do?"

"I am going to do my job and protect James."

"Then please go. I can see my door from here. I'll be fine."

He nodded looking relieved and rushed off.

I was glad that at least James would have someone watching his back. I walked to my rooms and said hello to my guards who were standing straighter than I had ever seen them. A small pang of guilt resonated in my heart when I noted Egan's absence.

I opened the door to my room and walked straight to my balcony doors for some air. With the guilt of Egan's death and my worry for James on my mind, I couldn't just sit in my room. A breeze was my only hope at relaxing. I pushed my balcony door ajar and froze with my hand on the knob.

From my view I saw a young man stacking hay against the wall behind the stables. The pile was nearly to the top of the wall, which was unusual. I stepped out onto my balcony for a better look. This was an odd sort of thing to be doing, especially with rain clouds ready to burst at any moment.

The young man put down his pitchfork and picked up a large coil of rope. It was tied in a circle at one end. He picked that end up and swung it high up around his head and let go. I watched it fly up and over the wall. He tied the rope off on the edge of the stables. Finished with his work he stood back staring expectantly at the wall.

What was he doing? He looked calm, almost bored. I decided I had better go inside to alert my guards to his odd actions when he lurched to attention. Something made the rope go taut. I darted back to my balcony railing. Someone in a long, black cloak appeared at the top of the wall. The person was holding onto the rope. I watched as another figure appeared behind the first and another. The first balanced on the wall for a moment, and jumped into the piled hay. The others began to follow. I counted ten men before I wrenched my eyes away. They'd be at the castle in only a few moments.

I raced through my room, threw open my door, and darted into the hall. "Quickly! Send someone to tell James they are getting in behind the stables," I shouted, but there was no one to receive the message except Roland—who was standing over the bodies of my two guards.

I yelped and turned toward my door, but Roland grabbed my arm and yanked me back toward him. "You know the nice thing about working in pairs is that there is always someone around to bail you out. Drumund the stable boy took more time than I would like, but he did not abandon me. He slipped me a key to my cell this morning. Come on, Lady A, we don't want to be late."

"Late for what?" I asked, the sting of Roland's betrayal hitting me anew with the return of my memories. I remembered how much James trusted his knights. How much Dan had trusted them.

"Your appointment with Manic," he said slapping the side of his sword against my back. I crumpled at the force of the blow. "He's not one to forgive a snitch like you." Roland pushed me forward and pointed the tip of his sword at my back. "He doesn't forgive anyone easily. Manic was mad that I failed him. So mad he nearly had my partner slit my throat in the cells, but instead he is offering me one more chance. A chance I will not squander."

I opened my mouth to scream, but he stuffed a dark cloth into my mouth. I gagged, but he yanked me to my feet and shoved me forward. "Be a good girl and walk nicely. Don't expect James to save you. He's a little busy."

He pulled my arm to his side and towed me down the hall. I had to warn James about the men sneaking into the castle. I had to get away from Roland. *But how?* I tried to pull away from him. He only held on tighter making my arm burn. He led me down the servant's staircase and down a long hall. Sounds of fighting echoed from the other end of the hall. "It's begun," hooted Roland.

Just before we took our last steps in the hall a black-cloaked figure appeared in front of us. My heart started beating faster as his cloak fell around his shoulders and the red patch with Manic's sign met my eyes.

Not another one.

He was breathing as if he had just climbed a mountain in full armor. He was leaning heavily on something but seemed to be chuckling slightly under his dark hood. Roland groaned.

"What are you doing here, Drumund. How many times do I have to tell you that I know what I am doing? I can handle this. Follow your instructions and go about your tasks at the stables and leave me to mine."

The cloaked mans hand moved and a crutch came forward. He blundered toward us with such slow shaky steps he must have been severely crippled. It couldn't have been Drumund.

"Well that's the funny thing about me Roland, I have never been good at following the rules."

Roland and I simultaneously gasped.

"Now, let go of my sister." Dan threw back his hood and drew his sword

Roland's sword quivered as he shoved me behind him. "Dan. You were dead."

"No, but I let you think that."

"We saw Manic toss your limp body into The Pit. No one has ever come back from there."

"Like I said, I don't like to follow the rules." Dan looked down at me. "Run."

I yanked the cloth out that Roland had shoved into my mouth. "Dan, how? I don't …"

"Get out of here!" yelled Dan. "Go find the queen and Princess Iree, they are in danger. Go! Now!"

I obeyed but I didn't want to leave him. Dan was alive. My brother was alive. I skirted past the two men holding their swords at the ready, until I was behind Dan.

"Don't go far, Lady A. Your brother really will be dead in a matter of a minute."

"Don't underestimate me, Roland."

"I never have," Roland spat as he lunged forward.

Dan blocked his attack and smirked. "No, you always have."

Burying my worry for my brother I raced down the hall, to find the queen.

Chapter 23

~Lady A~

I ran towards the entrance hall. My plan was to race up the steps and try their rooms first. Dan was right, if Manic was here the queen and Iree were both in grave danger.

I had to warn them.

I skidded into the entryway. At the sound of footsteps approaching I dove behind a chair. Two of Manic's men were pulling Iree and the queen down the stairs. I was too late. They had tied the queen's wrists together, but the other man held Iree's wrist. She was frozen with terror.

My heart ached for her as I remembered what it felt like to be so scared, I could hardly move.

Not Iree. Not sweet Iree. This would destroy her. Hurt her beyond belief. Hurt her in ways only I understood.

I didn't want Iree to feel that way any longer than she had to. I didn't want this day to change her life in a damaging way and affect her forever. I didn't want her to live in fear like I had. But what could I do?

A large silver vase sat on the table beside me. My arms began to shake and my blood began to race in my veins. I looked at Iree's trembling chin and back at the vase. *You only have to be brave for a moment,* I heard my brother say in the back of my mind. *Just one moment.*

They were only a step away when I jumped to my feet, grabbed the vase, and swung it with all of my might at the man holding Iree. I hit him square in the head and he dropped Iree to the ground.

With some kind of crazy strength, I didn't even know existed within me, I raised the vase again and hit the man holding the queen. I grabbed Iree's arm and the three of us raced out of the hall and into the first room we found. It was the courtiers' room.

We slammed the door closed and together we pushed a chair in front of it. I quickly untied the queen's hands. "They came out of nowhere," she said tearfully. Iree nodded her wide eyes still on the door.

"Not nowhere. Drumund the stable boy helped them over the wall. Roland helped as well. He escaped. They did this."

"You must be mistaken!"

"I wish I were. I was in my room and I saw Drumund letting Manic's men over the wall. Do you know if James …"

"No, we haven't heard anything. But the men who took us laughed about us being easier to corner than the prince."

A loud bang, like someone being slammed against the door, made all three of us jump. Iree screamed and curled into her mother.

"We've got to hide," I whispered. "Maybe if they don't see anyone in here, they will assume we escaped somewhere else."

Iree and her mother hid in a small wardrobe in the corner. I slipped under a table with a long cloth. The banging grew louder. We had settled in place for only a moment when the door burst open.

The man who had been haunting my dreams, stepped into the room followed by six others. The hair on my arms raised and I shivered. His wild, orange hair twisted out like an electrocuted lion's mane, and his black eyes flashed as he took in the room.

Manic.

"Come out little chicks," he clucked. "We know you're in here. We saw you."

I felt myself stiffen as his black cloak brushed past the table I was under as he walked further into the room.

Manic plopped down on one of the soft chairs and nestled his back against the cushions. "Find them," he instructed with a snap of his fingers. The six other men who had followed him into the room scattered.

Manic put his arms behind his head and kicked off his boots. The stench smelled like blood mixed with a waste pit.

"Ladies, if you're thinking that dear William or James will come bounding through the door, you are wrong. I have them well occupied. Today's the day Ladies. The day I take back my kingdom. I've waited my whole life for this. And you know what? I am tired of waiting. By this evening, I will be the one sitting on the throne with a gold crown on my head. And I'll be ordering the death of the so-called 'royal family' along with all those who said I couldn't do it. Or who don't think that I deserve it."

A pair of muddy shoes halted in front of the table I was hiding under, and I stopped breathing. The cloth lifted and coarse hands grabbed me and pulled me out. He roughly dragged me forward and pushed me down into a chair across from Manic.

Manic's face split into a devilish smile. My throat constricted. "Ah, the infamous Lady A, so nice of you to join me. Where are the other two?" I looked away from him to the floor. "Come on now, help a fellow out. I fought hard to get where I am. I deserve it and I deserve people who will obey my every command the moment I command them."

I said nothing and kept my head turned. Manic rose from his seat, and I held my breath. His dirty, sweaty hands grasped my chin and he forced my face around. I nearly gagged as his warm, rotting breath hit my face. "I can see why James is so interested in you. Perhaps if you are good, I will spare your life and you can still have a place on the throne." I recoiled and Manic laughed his lion-like laughter.

"The problem is, Lady A, that you are not enough for me to win. I can see James giving up his kingdom for you, but not William.

I need the other two women as well. Tell me where they are." Saliva dripped and gathered in the corners of his mouth as if he was about to devour his favorite food. I felt my skin prickle as every muscle in my body constricted.

I was not letting Iree anywhere near this hideous monster. A small amount of determination was lit inside of me. I let it grow; bubbling up until it filled me. I didn't know how to fight him. I couldn't use a sword. But I was going to fight nonetheless. Iree needed me too.

I looked around the room for some kind of idea. Manic followed my gaze hoping I was about to reveal the queen and Iree to him. But I didn't let my eyes linger anywhere near them.

The dark green leaves of the maze gardens outside the windows caught my eye. And I remembered James saying that the yellow stones led to the center. I was sure Roland had been a good spy, but not that good. If I could lead Manic away maybe he would get lost in there. Maybe I could trap him, until help arrived.

I had to try. I had to do this for Iree. I just needed a way to escape. But there was nothing. Nothing to grab, nothing to kick over, nothing at all but Manic's own rank smelling boots.

Shouting and the sound of swords clanging outside our door gave me what I needed. When Manic turned his head away from me to yell at his men, I reached down, grabbed his stinking boots, and flung them at his head. He fell down to a knee and slowly turned around his murderous eyes on mine. His eyes flashed red in the torchlight and his lips curled into a snarl. I jumped out of my seat and ran for the maze gardens—faster than I ever had run in my life.

Manic tore after me yelling foul curses into the wind. But I knew that without his boots he was sure to run a little slower than usual. I didn't look back as I turned into the maze or else my fear would have crumbled me. "Yellow stones, yellow stones," I mumbled as I ran down the path. I kept my eyes looking for the yellow stones and tried not to pay attention to the labored breathing behind me.

I lost my footing for a moment, scrambled back up to my feet, and whipped around a corner without thinking. Before I knew it, I was racing along a path without any yellow stones.

"You will pay for that act of defiance!" seethed Manic behind me. "Stop fighting your fate. I command you to stop!"

I kept running.

"You dare disobey the rightful king," he yelled. "I will not tolerate that. You will die, Lady A, and by my hand."

"Not if I can prevent it!" yelled James from somewhere behind us.

My heart leapt, but he sounded far enough away that I couldn't stop running. I turned down a straight path that lead to a small square garden. I dove behind a contoured bush, holding my sides. It wasn't much of a hiding place but it was enough to make Manic stop and look for me. He bent over half way and breathed heavily.

James ran into the garden. For a moment I was sure he would run Manic through and end this right then but Manic turned and blocked his blade. "I knew you'd come for her," Manic laughed. "The prince always follows his Lady."

"True, Manic, and that's why we also always have a happy ending."

"Not today!" shouted Manic raising his sword. Manic fought with his brutish strength but James could hold his own. I hardly breathed watching them. I was so sure James was going to win that I screamed when I watched as he was flung backward onto the path. Manic looked around and abandoned James even though he was already scrambling for his sword. Manic's bloodthirsty cognizance only had one focus at that moment, me.

I jumped up from my hiding place and ran out of the square garden down the nearest path. I quickly turned another corner at my soonest opportunity and nearly slammed into a dead end. I fell to the ground with my breath coming in gasps. This was it. Manic had caught me and James wasn't close enough.

I spun around and sure enough Manic dove for me. I tried to scramble out of the way, but he grabbed my arm and flung me to my knees in front of him like a shield.

He yanked a dagger out of his belt and put the tip of it to my jaw. I stiffened not daring to move even a little. James skidded to a halt in front of us with his sword in his left hand. I could see his right arm was bloody, through the torn sleeve.

Manic started laughing. "That's right, James, this will be my kingdom."

"Let her go, she has nothing to do with this. This is our fight," said James, taking a slow step forward.

"On the contrary, common citizen," he spat pressing the tip of the dagger into my jaw.

I gasped as the tip of his dagger hit bone and held as still as I could through my trembling.

James froze as Manic laughed again. "She means something to you, so she means something to me." I felt lightheaded as I watched a droplet of blood fall and land on my skirt.

"She is the reason that you are going to swear to me that you will give up your 'right' to the throne." Manic forced my face up.

I found myself staring at James. But he was looking past me right at Manic. "I mean right now!" Manic yelled.

James looked up toward the cloudy sky and nodded.

"No," I yelled as Manic cackled, but his laughter turned to a gasp of pain as someone jumped down on him from the top of the hedge. Manic drug his dagger down my jaw in what felt like an attempt to slit my throat as he was pulled backwards.

I clamped my hands on my stinging jaw as I fell forwards, but James caught me before I hit the ground.

"Lady A," said James, brushing my hair back. "Can you talk?"

"Ouch, ouch," was all I could manage to say. He pressed his warm hand against mine on my jaw.

"Richard? Dan?" He called.

"We got him, James."

I looked sideways through my hair in time to see Dan with his crutch and Richard dragging an unconscious Manic past us.

"My sister?" asked Dan.

James gently removed my hand, and I shuddered at the redness I saw there. "She will be fine," said James, pressing his own hand against the wound.

"Yeah, and sporting an awesome scar," said Dan as he and Richard dragged Manic away.

"Only a brother would say such a thing," James called after him.

"Now you know it's me for sure," he said as they rounded the corner. "Not a ghost like you thought at first."

"To be fair you did appear out of no where and join in the fight," called James, lightly tucking my hair behind my ear. "Come on, let's get you inside."

"Give me a moment, please." I was shaking, and I couldn't stop. James pulled me into his arms and held me until the shaking slowed and my breathing was closer to normal.

Gently he pressed a kiss to my forehead. The rest of my shaking faded away. He leaned closer his cheek resting against mine. "I love you, Lady A," he whispered in my ear.

Warmth filled my chest and I held onto him tighter. "Alora,"
I said softly.

"What?"

I pushed away from him just enough to see his face. "Alora,"
I repeated.

His face broke out into a smile as his other hand settled on
the other side of my face. Closing the short distance between us,
James pressed his lips to mine. The warmth spread through me from
my very core to the tips of my fingers. I threw my arms around him
deepening the kiss. He released me a moment later and leaned his
forehead against mine. "I love you, Alora."

"Are you sure? Apparently, I am a terrible tease."

He laughed and kissed me again.

Chapter 24

~Lady A~

I shouldn't have felt nervous walking down to breakfast the next morning, but I did. Everything was different. Manic was no longer trying to overthrow the kingdom, Dan was alive, and my memories were back. I was walking the halls of the castle as Alora, not Lady A. This was something I had honestly thought I would never do.

I stopped with my hand on the door when I heard voices.

Dan groaned loudly. "All right, you've convinced me, I will tell you. Manic didn't take my unwillingness to kill my sister well. After a good beating, he had me dragged back to his hideout near Lake Delmar to make an example out of me. He thought he had killed me and threw me into what he called The Pit. I woke up there sometime after they all left. I was hurt pretty bad.

It took me ages to get out of that dilapidated hovel he called home. I didn't have a horse and had to half crawl my way to Avern. I didn't think I was going to make it to Saris and honestly was about to give up when Charles the innkeeper found me."

"You're kidding."

"No."

"They patched me up. Told me all about how much they liked my sister and offered to sneak me into Saris. I didn't feel much like hobbling on my own so I accepted. I hid in the back of their cart and came out only in the shadow of the castle walls."

"I can believe it," laughed James. "Wendy and Charles should be given a medal or something."

Dan laughed, "Yes, it's rightly deserved for pulling Alora out of the river. Let alone what they did for me."

"I should almost knight him for saving the woman I love."

"Careful, James, that's my sister you're talking about," laughed Dan.

"I thought you had already given me your approval."

"Yes, but has she given you her approval?"

"I think so."

My cheeks grew hot and I turned away from the door only to see Iree walking my way. I was sad to see that the events of the night had taken some of her usual bounce. Her eyes lit up when she saw me though, and before I knew it, I was pulled into the tightest hug her little arms could give me.

"What are you doing here?" she asked, her smile half as bright as usual. I wasn't having that.

I smiled slyly and whispered, "Eavesdropping."

Iree giggled, put a finger to her lips, and peered around the door. She took a step back and gave me a slightly annoyed look. "On my brother and your brother?"

"Yes, so?"

She scrunched up her nose. "Are they really that interesting?"

I laughed. "Maybe not to you."

She rolled her eyes and held out her hand I took it, and together we walked into the room.

James's face split into a smile. He rose from his chair and came to offer me his good arm.

"May I escort the ladies to a seat?"

"Why, of course," I said as Iree giggled at her brother. I looked at Dan who winked at me.

"How are you feeling, Dan?" I asked after James helped me into my seat.

"So much better now. Madge is a miracle worker. And It looks like my crazy plan actually paid off," he said tossing a berry into the air and catching it in his mouth. I turned to look at James who was shaking his head at his best friend.

"I'm sorry to tell you, Dan, that I don't think it was worth it," James said.

"Of course, it was. But next time we should have some contingency plans."

"Like what?" I asked.

"Like what to do if the spy gets caught. Or someone loses her memory."

James looked at me and we didn't have to say a word. We already knew we would never let Dan get into this kind of trouble again. Not ever.

"Where are the king and queen?" I asked.

"Dealing with the aftermath of Manic's attack."

"And Manic?" I asked even though I was afraid they would tell me that he had escaped yet again.

"We don't have to worry about him anymore," said James, taking my hand. "He is gone for good."

"We had better hurry and eat," said Iree, taking three quick bites in a row. "We all slept in and we are going to be late for court. We can't miss it. Mother said so. She said they would all want to hear about our adventures and how we defeated the bad guy."

All eyes slowly turned to me and I shook my head. "Oh no, no. I think I'll pass, thank you."

"Alora you have to come!" whined Iree through her bite of toast. "You're the one who finished him off in the end."

"I did nothing of the sort. I ran and he followed. Dan, Richard, and James did the actual defeating. Besides," I said fingering the stitches along my jaw. "I don't really feel up to answering questions."

I looked to Dan for help, but he shook his head, "I agree with them. Alora, it's time you stopped being afraid of court. You played a huge role in vanquishing the bad guy. You have no reason to be afraid."

I turned to James, but he smirked. "I think you should go, too."

I put down my cup. My stomach was suddenly fluttering, not in a good way.

I could see it in their eyes, all of them. They were not going to let me get away with not attending. Unless, I could hide in my room first. I stood and mumbled some nonsense about leaving something in my room. I made it to the doors of the dinning hall before James stopped me. Dan was limping right behind him.

"No way, Sister. We are taking you down there right now," Dan said as he limped the rest of the way to the door. He had won his fight with Roland but not without new injury. He linked his arm through mine and James took hold of my other one.

"I can't do this."

"Of course, you can. You beat Manic; you can face court," said Iree coming up beside us.

"Don't let your fear of court beat you any more," said James. "You are brave, beautiful, adventurous, and kind."

"Sweet, talented, and a woman of noble birth," added Dan.

"Besides," said James, raising my hand to his lips. "Dan and I will be at your side the whole time, we swear."

They both stared at me, and I could tell they wanted me to make the choice to go on my own. But I didn't want to. I didn't care that I had been brave yesterday. I didn't want to be brave today.

However, I knew if I turned away, they would continue their encouragement until I relented, and I would be going anyway. There was no way out of this. I wanted to like court, I really did. It was a part of my world that I had closed the door on forever, only to be opened again when I couldn't remember why I didn't want to be there. It would have to be a part of my world now that I was part of James's world. I took a deep breath and nodded.

"Great! Let's go."

Sandwiched between them, they marched me directly to the room I had feared since I was twelve. Add to that the memories of Manic and I gulped as they paused to open the door.

Iree danced through first and gave me her widest of smiles. I felt the corners of my lips turn up at her face as she passed us. That girl.

Dan leaned in and stopped the door from closing behind her. He pulled it open wide enough for the three of us to walk through together. I admit I would have pulled back, but I didn't want to knock Dan off of his feet. The murmur of voices stopped at our entrance as everyone stared. Frederick bounded in front of us.

"Welcome to the heroes who fought off the dreadful Manic and freed our lands forever of his horrific deeds." He dramatically bowed and the courtiers applauded.

Rosetta moved swiftly to our side and took James's other arm.

"Oh, my goodness, James. I was so worried when I heard. I thought you'd be injured." She spied his wrapped arm and gasped louder than was necessary. "Oh dear, your arm." She turned her eyes to me and stared directly at the stitches along my jaw line. She gasped dramatically again. "At least your perfect face wasn't marred like Lady A's."

Dan took a step toward Rosetta. James shook her arm off of his, both men quickly coming to my aid.

"Her name is Alora Albon. And you're not a good enough friend to call her Lady A," said James.

Rosetta's jaw fell open.

"Only her truest friends have that pleasure," added Dan. My heart leapt as they came to my rescue and unexpectedly the room felt less intimidating.

"We are friends," she said as she tried to grab James's arm again.

But this time I pulled him away. Her eyes burned into mine and I matched her intensity with my own stare.

"No, we're not. You made that perfectly clear yourself. And I don't wish to change that," I said as we moved away from her together into the crowd of anxious courtiers who wanted to hear every detail of our adventures. Rosetta stood where she was simmering.

"Nicely handled," James whispered, and I smiled. I definitely wouldn't have done that before. I felt myself slowly relax. Maybe Dan and James were right. Maybe I really was ready for this. Maybe I didn't have a reason to be afraid anymore. Maybe I could end up liking court—eventually.

After our tale had been told, Iree bursting into the conversation whenever she could, the crowd dispersed a little bit and I saw Rosetta whispering with Mariel in a corner. I wanted to say something to her, but didn't know what to say. 'No hard feelings' felt a little premature. 'I'm sorry for your loss' also didn't fit. And, 'James loves *me*', ha, a little too haughty. I decided that I would have to wait until I knew what to say.

"What would you say if we took a stroll in the gardens?" James asked me. I eyed Dan who was making a group of courtier's gasp with more of his own tale. "Don't worry he will be fine."

I looked at the crowd surrounding him and noticed they were all women. He was smiling and laughing. He looked like the ridiculous, joyful Dan I always knew.

"All right," I said. I gave Dan's arm a slight squeeze and he turned my way. "We are going to walk for a bit."

"Sounds good," he said with a wink and turned back to his crowd.

"He always was a people person," I said as James and I walked away.

"I know. The ladies are always vying for his attention. I don't know how he will deal with it all now."

"Now?"

"Now, that I am taking myself out of the running," he whispered in my ear as we walked out into the rose gardens.

I gasped dramatically, "Why would you do such a thing?"

"I was actually hoping you would help me out with that."

"Me?" I said attempting to look innocent. I epically failed. He laughed, and pulled me into his arms.

"Yes, you. I love you, my Lady A. Will you marry me?"

I laughed and I pushed him back. "Lady A?"

"It was the name you made up special for me, was it not?"

"It was," I said a smile peeking out.

"Then, my dear, Alora, it will always be special to us. So, Lady A, what do you say?"

"I say…I love you too James. I would love to become your wife."

He kissed me softly, and a warm shiver shot up and down my arms. A loud wailing sound spoiled the moment.

"No! James is *my* prince. I am supposed to marry him! He is in love with me," Rosetta screeched, her face as red as the trim on her dress.

"No, he never was," I said lacing my fingers with his.

She pursed her lips.

"And I never will be," James added holding me tighter.

With a very unladylike scream, she stormed off. James pulled me back into his arms and held me as we watched her stomp away toward Mariel. But the only words I was able to hear out of her vicious ranting was, "… get back at Alora for this."

They disappeared, and James reached into his pocket.

"I have something for you,"

I fully expected it to be a ring, but instead he pulled out a crumpled piece of paper. "This is for you; it has been next to my heart for two years." I unfolded it and smiled at the names written there. At the very bottom in new ink was scrawled *Alora*.

"Are you sure you want to give it up?"

"I don't have to guess anymore," he said. "But I thought you would like to have it."

"Thank you, but if you think you won't have to guess anything else with me you are sorely mistaken."

He laughed, "I look forward to it," he said, pulling me close for another kiss.

A few minutes later, we walked back into the courtier's room hand in hand. Rosetta jumped to life when she saw us. I guess she had been waiting for our return. She put on her best smile and sauntered over to Dan.

She shooed away a few of the girls who where fawning over him and sat right next to him. Dan acknowledged her as much as anyone else, but I knew that wouldn't discourage her.

"You know, we are going to have to watch out for Dan for forever," I said.

"I knew what I was getting into when I chose my best friend," James said as he kissed the top of my head. "And without him, I wouldn't have you. So, it's worth it."

I beamed pulling his arms around my waist. "Shouldn't we rescue him from Rosetta's clutches."

"Only if we have to, my love. Until then I am staying right here with you."

Acknowledgements

Always first and forever I have to thank my sweet husband who loves and supports my dreams. Who takes our kids on adventures while mommy writes. You are amazing John Shiels and I love you forever. Thank you for supporting me and for believing in me. You are also an invaluable proof reader.

I also want to thank my kiddos who helped color on my pages or had me trace your hands on my manuscript while I edited. Thanks for getting so excited with me when I told you about my stories and for understood that mommy has a dream to write books. Your support means the world to me. Love you all!

Huge thank you to my fantastic beta readers. Leah Knighton, Karen Adair, Alison Parkllan, Clarissa Miller, and Teya Peck. You all gave me the kick in the pants to cut over 50 pages of this book and rewrite them. For the better I might add. Thanks for all of your hard work and comments. You are all super amazing. Special thanks to Alison Parkllan who read it twice for me. Special thanks to Karen who told me where I needed to up the emotion and to make it messy. I needed to hear that. Also, a big thanks to Karen for letting me bug you with multiple what if and does this sound better moments.

Thank you to Alice Miller, Clarissa Miller, Jeremy Miller, Leah Knighton and to my wonderful friend Kim Ward who are always there for me when I need to hash something out. Kim you helped me feel like I finally got this story right even to the last words.

Thank you so much to my editors: Barbara Elkington, Cristine Garrison, and Brett Miller. You all truly made my story shine. Editors work hard you all! Thank you for all that you did and fixed. I needed you!

Thank you, Jeremy Miller, for my amazing original cover photo. You are the best! My new one is beautiful too.

Thank you to all those who love and keep encouraging me, who teach me and are patient with me.

Finally thank you to all my fantastic readers!! You rock! I hope you keep coming back for more. And there will be more coming soon!

About the Author

Cassie M. Shiels

Cassie has loved stories since she was little. Her love of writing started even before she could write words. She was one to be found, reading late into the night (wait, she still does that!), on the school bus or before she did her homework. In middle school she determined that she liked creating her own stories as much as she liked reading them; so, she decided she wanted to be an author and keeps working on making that dream come true with every story idea that bounds into her head.

For more about Cassie and her writing visit her website:
www.cassiemshiels.com

If you liked Lady A, please consider leaving a review on amazon.com, Goodreads, etc.

Like this book and want more. Check out my book TRICKED A free Novelette only for my newsletter subscribers.

What does a Foiled Prince and a Clever Witch have in common?
Revenge!
Find it on www.cassiemshiels.com

Her books:

A Princess Tale series

The Royal Spy (book 1)
Lady A (book 2)
The Prince's Decoy (book 2)

The Queens of Adelfa book series coming soon!

If you like sweet Romance please find my pen name Cassandra Shiels and check out those books as well. Find them at my website www.cassiemshiels.com

17636229R00146